THE MEASURE OF DARKNESS

LIAM DURCAN

THE MEASURE OF DARKNESS

BELLEVUE LITERARY PRESS
NEW YORK

First published in the United States in 2016 by
Bellevue Literary Press, New York

For information, contact:
Bellevue Literary Press
NYU School of Medicine
550 First Avenue
OBV A612
New York, NY 10016

Library of Congress Cataloging-in-Publication Data
is available from the publisher upon request.

Bellevue Literary Press would like to thank all its generous
donors—individuals and foundations—for their support.

The New York State Council on the Arts with
the support of Governor Andrew Cuomo and
the New York State Legislature

This project is supported in part
by an award from the National
Endowment for the Arts.

Book design and composition by Mulberry Tree Press, Inc.

Manufactured in the United States of America.
First Edition

1 3 5 7 9 8 6 4 2

paperback ISBN: 978-1-942658-04-7

ebook ISBN: 978-1-942658-05-4

For Thomas Durcan

THE MEASURE OF DARKNESS

Part I

I would like to see more clearly, but it seems to me that no one sees more clearly

—Maurice Merleau-Ponty

Prologue

It started with Martin recalling the surprise he'd felt when he first saw the house. He had expected to glimpse it from the end of the street, to have the luxury to appreciate it from a distance as he approached. But he hadn't seen it coming. He just looked up and there they were, the professor and Martin, his assistant, in front of Konstantin Melnikov's house on Krivoarbatsky Lane. After the bustle of the early-morning markets at the Arbat, in the center of old Moscow, the atmosphere of Krivoarbatsky Lane was more suitably subdued, dour in a predictable, Soviet way that had obviously lulled him.

Melnikov House was like nothing else on the street. Like nothing else he'd ever seen. It was two interlocking cylinders—truncated towers, really—with rows of small hexagonal windows honeycombing across its white facade. Professor Lanctot put down the duffel bag that held the camera equipment, and together they stood, staring at the building. It was warm. Martin had been warned that Moscow's spring weather was as unpredictable as Montreal's; wet snow was not uncommon this late in April, the tail end of a winter snapping one last time on the city. It was a threat seemingly acknowledged on the face of every Muscovite they'd met in the last week. A grim refusal to be caught out in one's hope. He looked over, to find Professor Lanctot attaching a lens to his camera, working quickly and silently, as though he were preparing to photograph an animal about to flee. Lanctot glanced at the light meter held in his outstretched hand.

"Tripod?" Martin said to Lanctot, doing his best to sound collaborative, having to settle for helpful.

Lanctot did not divert his gaze. *"Non. Merci."*

They were supposed to have met an interpreter at the hotel, but they'd chosen instead to leave early in order to get out and see the Arbat without an official chaperone. Lanctot had left a message at the desk of the hotel, asking whoever was sent by the embassy to meet them at the house. All this struck Martin as unnecessarily risky, but he had discovered that Lanctot was a different man since their arrival in Moscow, transformed from one of the fussier academics in the School of Architecture to a scholarly James Bond, newly unflappable and surprisingly resourceful, a man given to suddenly revising plans, which, in turn, caused the cultural attachés at the embassy to throw up their hands. All it took to liberate him was a repressive regime. And a house here on Krivoarbatsky Lane.

The problem with Lanctot's change in plan, of course, was that it meant no one was there to meet them; and without the bureaucratic approval—or the translation skills—of a government official, traipsing up the front walk and banging on the door was plainly out of the question. So they waited. After ten minutes, Lanctot collected his gear and gestured to Martin to follow to the other side of the building.

"You have to see it from the north. You'll see. Very impressive."

They walked together, wading through a yard overrun by a knee-high crop of nettles. He remembered the thrill of being there with Lanctot, even if he was little more than sidekick to a rogue scholar. He was twenty-two and traveling in Moscow, walking into the backyard of a house he'd already come to know, treading around the seminal work of an architect who had become mythic to him. They had spent the last ten days exploring the city, visiting and photographing Melnikov's other Moscow works, the Rusakov Club in the Sokolniki District and what remained of the Leyland bus garage, but, perhaps out of a newfound sense of showmanship, Lanctot had decided to save the house for last. Or maybe it was that he wanted to walk through the Arbat along the way, to study the setting for Melnikov's grand reorganization of the marketplace, which, like so many of the architect's other plans, never came to fruition. Perhaps that was the lesson that needed to be learned before seeing the house.

Whatever Lanctot's motives, the anticipation of seeing the structure was heightened by the promise of an audience with the great architect in his house. Konstantin Melnikov himself. This alone was worth the travel and the visas and the embassy's having to vet their plans. Martin imagined tea with the architect and his wife in the caverns of the house, along with a vague expression of kinship and some sort of tearful recognition of how far they'd traveled. It embarrassed him now, but yes, he'd expected a measure of gratitude from Melnikov, along with the tea.

They maneuvered around to the back of the property, nestled more tightly between the neighboring houses than he would have expected. He tried to look at the house, the northern elevation, which Lanctot had found so worthy of special attention.

But something was wrong: He could not find the house. It seemed to be there and yet it had vanished. And then he looked at Lanctot, and Lanctot had no face. It was like studying the details of a dream. (He knew it was Lanctot simply because it could not have been anyone else, faceless there beside him, scrambling through the nettles).

Now he could summon only a remembered fragment from inside the Melnikov house, a curious sensation, not related to space or light at all—just the taste of tea, black tea without sugar, served to Lanctot and him as they sat in the main room for a wordless audience with the great man, who had eventually shepherded them in from his front yard, an act less of Russian hospitality than Soviet pragmatism, escorting them into his house and away from whatever surveillance they might have attracted. He remembered the tea. The formal pressure of a china cup's rim against his lower lip. He remembered the house as beautiful, but this, he thought, must have been a memory, or an assumption, because he could not see it, could not recall the house in its entirety. Melnikov House had not vanished as much as dissolved in the difficulties of looking at it. Glare. Lens flare. Overexposure.

And now, more than thirty years after the visit, Martin found himself awakening in a different room—in a different world, really—both with their own relentlessly rectangular windows. He heard another patient across the hall cough. These were morning sounds. It must be morning. He tried to move, but his body objected in that now familiar twisting, visceral way. But none of that mattered. Until this moment, Martin had been unsure whether he could summon any detail of the house. Now he was certain that, in some vital way, it still existed in him. He was certain it would return in full.

Professor Lanctot had died ten years earlier, Melnikov had been dead more than thirty. But this amended memory lived. The memory announced itself to him there in the hospital bed. And thinking about all of this now, he felt he understood for the first time a pilgrim's view of the world. Imperceptible truth. Beauty that escaped his ability to describe it. Faith.

Chapter 1

Concentrate on the linear. The linear is all you have.

Dr. Feingold had said it weeks ago. It was after a session—their last session, as it turned out—when she came to visit him, sneaking up on him in that way he suspected was at least partially deliberate. She sat down in a chair in the corner of the room. Martin listened to the deliberateness of a body's weight being placed into one of those institutional chairs. The grudging rebuttal of the chair. He remembered searching for her, his focus rummaging through the shadows and joists of sunlight, until suddenly she was there.

"It's dark in here," he said, trying to position himself so that she would sit still in his field of vision.

"The lighting is fine, Martin."

They spoke for a while, like they always did, in a way that managed to flatter and perplex him at the same time. She was intelligent. And attractive, he thought, although this impression came from nothing more than her voice, the therapeutic deliberateness in pronunciation, the change in pitch at the end of a sentence, which he suspected was professionally calculated, an allowance for him to say more than he initially wanted. Her voice reining him in and then giving him room.

His vision clutched at a sliver of reflected light that marked a looped earring. From there, he found an earlobe, then the tight ringlets of her hair. A long march toward Dr. Meredith Feingold began, the angle of her jaw that fed the chin and from there the French curve of her lower lip, followed from its fullness to where it tapered into a point. Trying to understand her eyes was a different matter; he was forever chasing something in the eyes that confused him, that made him arrive back at a starting point. Instead, he'd found himself focused on detached physical facts. The sound of her breathing. Blink rate. Vital signs. But it went beyond this; he was most drawn to the little wall of flesh that made up the arch of her nostril. While it was a nondescript region of only a couple of square centimeters, he'd recently been given to thinking about it quite incessantly, wondering whether this territory of Feingold had ever been pierced with a small metal stud when she was in university or kissed or even considered in passing by those who held her dear, if this beautiful structure had ever been subjected to the type of scrutiny that he'd given it—he viewed this as a sign that heralded recovery, because for the first time he could imagine Feingold in the past, as having a past, or as a person outside of her professional duties. A trail of her, the wake of a personality. These imaginings seemed to explain her better than her features, which, despite his obsessively cataloging them every time he saw her, could not be combined into anything resembling a recognizable face.

He looked forward to seeing her every day after physio- and occupational therapy. But other than his fractures, which were healing and were none of her concern anyway, he felt fine and couldn't understand why she was so interested in his case. During their first visits, he was under the impression that she had been sent to help him deal with the aftermath of the accident, but he soon discovered, to his relief, that Dr. Feingold had no interest in talking about the psychic injuries the crash had inflicted. As for his memories of the accident itself, he had been wiped clean.

No flashbacks or second-guessing in the moments leading up to the accident, just an amnestic void that stretched weeks before the impact. And while he was frustrated at having a gap in his life, at having no answer for the events leading up to the accident, he had recently understood that having no recollection meant being spared, both living through and reliving, the experience of the trauma. If he could not recall, it was not beyond him to at least imagine the terror of that moment of oncoming headlights, the panic that would come with swift imminence, the helplessness. On the occasion of their last meeting, in his room on the third floor of the Dunes Rehabilitation Center, on the outskirts of Burlington, Vermont, the conversation turned, as it always seemed to do, to his work. Feingold, famously—at the Dunes anyway—was from "New York," and she was professionally vague about the reasons for her recent New England exile, leaving him to infer that it was part of some sort of exercise in relationship building (a partner trying to scrape out tenure in the classics department at the local university, he surmised). It had to be that; a move to a backwater rehab palace like the Dunes to further one's own career would have been nothing more than poor judgment. It took no time to discover—even for someone staggering out of the debris field of his own brain injury—that, as a result of the move, Feingold was insatiably nostalgic for New York. She was forever wanting to know more about the buildings she had grown up with and had so loved, so he indulged her, and for hour after hour, in what was likely billed as psychotherapy, they talked about architecture. She would start with a building, asking him to tell her about it. Typical stuff, tourist stuff: the Chrysler, the Seagram, the Flatiron—the first thing he did there was correct her: The Flatiron was properly called the Fuller Building, he said, after the company that first built it and once resided there, and went on to describe his favorite characteristics of architect Daniel Burnham's work, that sheer wall of limestone he had placed at the base of the Fuller. As he spoke to Feingold, Martin remembered taking his daughter Susan to see the wall, to touch it, on a trip to New York the summer before her last year of high school. She had been talking about her future—industrial-design studies or architecture—and he had wanted to take her to New York, he could admit now, to sway her decision. He felt that she needed to see the buildings, Burnham's wall, up close. But it was also the summer after he and Sharon had separated, and the trip was mired in a wordless fog of recriminations that no amount of facade touching could hope to dispel. He doubted Susan would remember the trip or the building now, much less appreciate his motives.

He could feel the texture of the stone as he talked about the Fuller Building, the simplified lines rising from the fussy French Renaissance details of the building's base. Those beautiful planes of limestone, he told Feingold, were pure Daniel Burnham, the Chicago architect who built it, a man whose work was felt to have lost its special flourishes after the death of his partner, John Wellborn Root. He told her he thought Burnham was better for the loss.

But on this last occasion, their conversation was different. He turned to Dr. Feingold when he heard himself talking, speaking digressively but saying nothing insightful, like a tour guide who could see the details of his day's journey with his eyes closed. This thought made Martin stop, as though being patronized was something novel, an act that demanded to be appreciated in silence.

"Go on," she said.

"I'm tired. The light is bad."

"Tell me what you think is wrong with you."

"Boredom. Fluorescent lighting. I want to go." He watched her. She had been blinking every three to four seconds, gestures flaring a little more freely, the background noise of human movement turned up. Engaged Feingold. Maybe just caffeinated Feingold. And then he sensed her stiffening. "If you ask me, my visual memory is impaired. I can't hold things in my memory."

She asked him to imagine walking north up Fifth Avenue, which he immediately recognized was an excuse to get him to describe the Guggenheim. She asked what he could see, what he remembered, and he accepted the dare, giving her a nice little impromptu lecture about late-period Wright, even surprising himself with how well he could describe the building itself.

Then she asked him to visualize walking up past the museum, say to Ninetieth Street, and to turn and view Fifth Avenue looking toward the south. She asked him to tell her what he could see. It was as if he were in a different city, that he'd somehow gotten lost in the foliage of Central Park, trapped in a crowd of tourists on the steps of the Met. Where was the Guggenheim? she asked, and he told her he was lost, and lied, saying that he hadn't been to New York recently, that he was working from memory. "The Guggenheim is there," she said, "but you're not looking for it," which was preposterous to him. "This is what we've been talking about; this is neglect," she said, trying to explain that he might never be the same.

Neglect. That curious word. A word she used to describe what the accident had done to him, taken from him. When he argued that he felt well, that he could feel himself becoming stronger, that perhaps the Dunes was a therapeutic place after all, she corrected him. She went over again how his right hemisphere had been contused in the accident and because of this he was not aware of his deficits; *the key part of the deficit was not to be aware of its extent.*

Feingold said that when he was looking south down Fifth Avenue, the Guggenheim was not just trapped in darkness; it had ceased to exist. He would never look for it, so he would never find it. He argued that it was his visual memory that was impaired, but Feingold said it wasn't just the Guggenheim: Every morning he ate only what was on the right side of his plate, and did he notice that Szandor, the orderly, had to complete his shave every morning by removing a day's worth of stubble from the untouched left cheek?

He nodded, because there was really no way to argue with someone like Feingold. Feingold was power here. Instead, she explained that the nervous system did three things: It received and collated sensory information, created hypotheses about the world, and then tested these hypotheses. The accident had made him unable to ask questions about certain parts of his world. Neglect, she said, meant that the Guggenheim disappeared, and would keep disappearing, along with the East Side, along with everything to one side of him.

Martin told her he was tired, that he couldn't concentrate, and tried to give the impression that he didn't feel like talking about New York architecture if it was only going to be used to humiliate him in some way. But Feingold was not leaving.

"I'm really exhausted, Dr. Feingold." It had come to that, he thought, appealing to her sympathy for reprieve. She just sat, unmoved.

"I wanted to speak to you about the therapists' opinion," she said.

Ah, the therapists. The Dunes was world-renowned for its therapist-to-patient ratio. It's what got Brendan, his brother, to pay to have him assessed and air-ambulanced down here after he was discharged from the trauma ward of a hospital back in Montreal. Four months of therapists: speech and language, art and music, occupational and physio, earnest missionaries forever intent on rescuing an apostate like him from the baser pleasures of food or sleep, always dragging him off to one of their rooms forested with implements whose uses he could not fathom.

They'd had meetings, Feingold said. *Multidisciplinary meetings.* Social workers and the floor's head nurse joining the fray every Tuesday and Friday morning.

He had come to realize the multidisciplinary discussions were the absolute highlights of the Dunes experience. He'd sat in on one a month before—a rare treat, and only at Feingold's insistence—and found the event to have a tone that alternated between an old-time revival meeting and an intervention for some poor drug-addicted cousin, with representatives of the different disciplines occasionally bristling at the presence of rival expertise, all jostling for input, so much worked-up goodwill in the room that it demanded to be used on somebody. *Multidisciplined.* It meant they felt you were too far gone to really get better, to get normal. It meant that their efforts would be recast. Less search and rescue, more recovery of the body.

When he spoke to Feingold after that meeting, he asked her what the initial feelings were, even though it was obvious to him. Feingold said she doubted he would ever work again. She paused and qualified her statement: not work at the same level anyway.

Plateau was now in his lexicon. A word from the occupational therapists and the doctors, part of his geography of newly diminished expectations.

"I think I know. But you still think I need more therapy."

"Well, with work you could be more functionally independent. You'll need a supervised setting for a while. But with some modifications, we could think about getting you back home. Without anyone there, it would be more difficult, naturally. And when that happens, eventually, you could do outpatient . . ."

He turned his head in her direction. They'd had this discussion before. He was unrealistic; he was in denial. He could walk, though; didn't that count for something? How many others could claim to have walked out of the Dunes? His wing of the Dunes hosted residents whose stories hadn't allowed them to come this far, shrieking, tremulous young men who'd lost their footing on a rooftop or whose motorcycle had found that infamous dream-ending, dream-beginning patch of wet pavement. Bed to bath, bath to chair, chair to bed. He could hear their lives triangulated in these short voyages, in the grunt and groan of the orderlies, whose efforts they needed to move at all. But that wasn't his life. That wasn't him.

He had come to believe that he was nothing to Feingold except the specifications of his condition. And the specs weren't good, definitely not up to code. His opinion, of course, was moot, whatever progress he made—and he got the feeling it could have been cartwheels or calculus—was nothing next to Feingold's opinion and the verdict of some committee in the hospital. In some ways, it was like he was starting out again as an architect, submitting a proposal invested with everything he was as an architect, only to suffer the group whims of group taste, always maintaining that rejection didn't hurt, never admitting the grievous sting.

The roomful of multidisciplinarians saw him as a man struggling to operate a toaster and falling down stairs and, if they didn't intercede, planning buildings that would be doomed to collapse and crush everything, including their reputations. Feingold wanted the best for him, to keep him off the floor and far from the toaster, and in a way, he appreciated this. He respected her for it. But at the same time he wanted to reach out and put a finger into that looped earring, to lean over and whisper that she knew nothing of him. *How dare she.* She couldn't know what he had, what he was. She couldn't know what they were taking away.

He could still talk about buildings, she said. Maybe, with what he knew, he could write or teach. She had spoken to his partners, Feingold said. She knew he'd written articles. He could feel himself grimacing at the thought of Jean-Sebastien or Catherine "confiding" to Feingold about him.

"I don't want to write. I'm still an architect."

Feingold nodded and told him she enjoyed listening to him talk provenance, about the decisions made to achieve an effect in his buildings and in others. She placed an object on the table and told him that she wanted him to record his thoughts, to listen to the playback every night. He touched the object on the desk, a density and size that identified it as a piece of electronic equipment, a similar heft and feel to the digital recorder he had used before.

"Was this mine?"

"No. It's new. I thought you could use it."

"Where'd mine go?"

"I don't know. Maybe it's at home. Maybe it was in the car. This one works. . . ."

He ran his thumb over the narrow edge of the object and felt what must have been the RECORD button, invariably there, always on the narrower edge of the instrument, designed for a thumb to work it like a rosary bead. "Testing, testing."

The PLAYBACK button was more mysteriously located, lost among a minor archipelago of other-functioned buttons, but simply living in an era that demanded mastering successive generations of cell phones and PDAs and BlackBerry devices had trained his thumbs in ways that he could not describe or understand. Three tries until he heard his voice, testing, testing. Testing him.

He smiled; a machine they trusted him with. This, he understood, was the linear that Feingold was asking him to accept, the only connection he had left to his life, the only lifeline they would allow him. Feingold was making her case for what he would be permitted. He should be grateful to be alive; he should be grateful to be allowed this much. Testing, testing.

But he wasn't grateful. He wanted to tell her this was theft. A story about a building was nothing without the building itself—a process that he was being told was now forever beyond him. Without him being at the helm, his practice, which he had built and fostered and sacrificed for, was in jeopardy. When he founded it, his firm had been nothing, a small shop happy to exist on renovation work and retrofitting municipal buildings, and now, because of his work and his name, F/S+H was competing for the sort of projects that were the preliminary markers of a career of distinction. The endowed museum extension. The named research pavilion. And then came the consulate. It was happening. The next ten years were supposed to be a culmination, not spent playing mind games finding the goddamned Guggenheim.

He wanted to shout at her that they owed him more than this, more of a chance. But you don't tell this to people like Feingold, he reminded himself; you don't tell her about how you can understand space more fully with your eyes closed, the brief moments when you're aware of so much, when space seems full and more beautiful than before. They would never understand. They'll give you the linear and you will take the linear.

He called for the orderlies—Szandor, or the other guy, who was smaller than Szandor—to help get him into bed, and that's when she started to go on about the next few weeks at the Dunes, how they would consolidate their cognitive rehab program for him. He had already tuned her out, choosing instead to repeat the phrase because the sound of the words, sounding like a means of escape, a method of rehabilitation completely within his own power, had started to please him. *Concentrate on the linear.*

Chapter 2

"Dr. Fallon?"

Brendan Fallon stopped and slowly turned around in the atrium lobby of the Dunes Rehabilitation Center at the sound of his name. It had been more than a year since he'd retired as a veterinarian, and hearing his name and former title here, in a place where no one should know what he did, made him briefly uncomfortable at the thought of coming face-to-face with a former employee or client whose pet's name he would not recall.

Meredith Feingold was waving at him from behind the reception desk, the clattering of bracelets clustered on her right forearm accentuating the gesture, making it seem more urgent, as if that were possible. The sound made by her jewelry stopped as her gesture fluidly morphed into the less emphatic one of beckoning him back from the exit. Several others in the lobby also stopped and looked back at the desk. Perhaps they were Dr. Fallons, as well, Brendan thought, a lobby full of astrophysicists and chiropractors and pediatricians, distant relatives he'd never met. But Feingold was looking at him, and so the others were dismissed to rejoin their faux Fallon lives and doctoral careers. Brendan waved back and reflexively turned his wrist to check the time, which was odd, as he was in no rush, but less odd than the fact that he wasn't wearing a wristwatch in the first place.

What he knew of Meredith Feingold came mostly from

Martin, whose opinion seemed more dependent on his cycling moods than on her therapeutic performance. Martin was running through a difficult patch, and his current complaint was that all Feingold's questions were rhetorical. Brendan had briefly come across Dr. Feingold several times during his brother's stay at the Dunes, a nod and a polite smile as he dropped Martin off at her office or picked him up after the session was over. It was a novelty now to simply see her away from a door frame. Organic, free-range Feingold. She took a step toward him and shook his hand, the type where the otherwise-free hand came up to join the little hand hug at the last second and was deployed, Brendan thought, to convey some deeper emotional meaning than just "Hello" but was forever wasted on people like him who overanalyzed handshakes.

"I'm sorry for disturbing you, Dr. Fallon, but I wondered if we could talk about your brother," Feingold said, not waiting for a response before disengaging from the handshake and sweeping her right arm back to show him the way to her office. Rhetorical, Brendan thought, impressed that at least Martin had been paying attention.

Down a corridor and into the Psychology Department he was led, past the threshold of that familiar door frame, and shown a seat. Feingold opened a file folder that had been sitting on her desk. She must have been waiting for him at the front desk. The office was decorated perfectly, hints of eclecticism but impeccably tidy, Brendan thought. On the wall, just above her left shoulder was a framed print of New York, one of those iconic photos of an eagle-headed gargoyle projecting out from the facade of the Chrysler Building into the abyss of a distant Manhattan. Feingold noticed him looking.

"Martin tells me that you live in New York."

"Upper East Side. Mid-Seventies."

"Nice. How do you find Vermont?"

"It's so nice and bucolic, I want to throw up." It pleased him to see her smile.

Martin is impulsive. Martin is amnestic. Martin has left a lot of people angry at him. Martin is a person who made plans for great buildings that were occasionally built. Martin is a mystery to me. Brendan thinks of all the things that his brother is and was, because he finds the list makes the discussion he is inevitably going to have with Feingold easier. He had gone through similar mental lists, the crib sheets of the unprepared, on those rare occasions when he was cornered into a parent-teacher conference for one or the other of their boys, trying to project some form of parental insight that could pretend to complement Rita's. The list, he thought, was preparation, a way to reduce the anxiety of being overmatched, and this was necessary to combat the glade of perspiration blossoming in that area between his shoulder blades and the sense of general abdominal discomfort. Now he understood why he was looking at the watch that was never there, an effort to create in Feingold's mind a sense of his being imposed upon, that he was a person whose clock was ticking and the meeting, as a courtesy, should be both brief and held on his terms.

"So you're the family," Feingold said.

"I am," Brendan replied, and tried to smile innocuously as possible, resisting the impulse to tilt his head.

"You're okay with that?"

"Okay with being family? I suppose I don't have any choice in the matter."

"Are you okay with being responsible for him, Dr. Fallon?"

"I wouldn't have been here every day for three months if I wasn't okay with it. I wouldn't have agreed to be his guardian if I wasn't comfortable. Besides, it's been mostly details and paperwork, a few visits back to Montreal to sign things. . . ."

"I think all of that is *admirable,*" Feingold said, and as she spoke the index finger of her right hand slowly moved across the surface of the piece of paper in front of her, stopping mid-line, mid-page. "Martin told me, during one of our conversations—outside the context of his sessions, of course—that you hadn't seen each other in almost thirty years."

"That's true."

"That must make everything more difficult for you."

"He's the one who's been in a coma. Everything else is sort of easy compared to that."

Meredith looked at him and smiled. "You don't like talking about this."

"I don't know what we're talking about, Dr. Feingold."

"I've found, in the course of my work, that people who are estranged are often estranged for a reason. There are often real and deeply felt reasons why people who grew up together move apart and stay away from each other—"

"Look, it's just pragmatism, Dr. Feingold. I have the time. My kids are grown and I'm retired. Martin's daughters are busy with their lives and our mother is almost ninety. He has one ex-wife who's overseas and another who didn't want anything to do with him *before* this. . . ."

"I understand that. I'm not talking about them, I'm talking about you, Brendan. In my experience, people who try to restart relationships under these circumstances are often expecting some resolution. That's a significant burden to place on a fragile relationship and especially on a person who is recovering from an injury."

"I'm here for my brother, that's all. And I'm fine, really, and I don't expect anything from this, except for him to get better. But I do appreciate your interest in my welfare."

Feingold turned over the page, and Brendan glanced down to see what looked to be a place for signatures. He felt the urge again to consult a clock but understood that in a psychologist's office all the clock faces would probably be turned away from the client.

"Martin wants to leave," Feingold said.

Brendan nodded. "He's been talking to me about that."

"His attention is better and his reading has improved, but the treatment team doesn't think that he's entirely ready to go."

"What do you think?"

"He's injured his right hemisphere and has what is called 'neglect.' It's hard to explain, but certain parts—the left side of his world—aren't normal."

Brendan nodded, "He's weak on the left and can't see very well on that side."

"It's more than that," Feingold said, and paused. The pen she was holding followed the tracks of a small elliptical doodle on a piece of scrap paper on the desk. "Have you ever had that experience where you learn about something, an event, or an artist, or a concept, and you're amazed that you had never heard of it? And then, of course, after the initial time you hear of it, you hear it referred to all the time; it's like you can't avoid it. But it hadn't existed for you before. It hadn't seemed possible. The odd thing is to realize how you were making opinions, not just unaware, but unaware you were unaware. Martin is unaware of his deficits, of his visual problems. His world seems full to him. Seamless, in many ways."

"Will this get better?"

"I don't know. I think I have to agree with the team, but I also think progress for him at the Dunes, in his current state of mind, will be difficult. . . ." Brendan knew what was coming, having shaped conversations like this all through his career, the niceties seguing into heartfelt discussions about an animal's welfare prior to the brass tacks of price points and the limits of care and waiver after waiver to be signed. But he appreciated her exquisite goddamned professionalism.

"The best solution, I think, if Martin really insists on leaving, for us as an institution . . . it would be best for us if he left 'against medical advice,' and for that we need you to sign that you knew about this decision and agreed to take full legal responsibility for him until he returned to Canada." With that, Feingold rotated the folder toward Brendan. "We can leave it undated for now."

"Sure. I have no problem with that," Brendan said, and, having had it ready and already used, quickly put his pen away.

It was Friday, now late afternoon, and the hallway of the Psychology Department was appropriately deserted. Brendan thought they would part ways at her office, expecting Feingold's customary offer to accompany him to the exit, countered by him politely declining and showing himself out—but after closing and locking the door to her office, she kept walking with him, the sound of their footsteps awkwardly twinned. She could do better with goodbyes, he thought.

"Before you go," she said without turning to face him, "I was wondering if you could give me a little advice. My dog, a Doberman—"

"How old?" he asked, the mystery of the protracted good-bye now explained, calling on whatever vestiges of professionalism he still had to suppress a look of annoyance.

"Betsy is four. Really healthy, but she fainted this morning."

"When's your next vet appointment?"

"In a few months."

He paused for a moment. "You should mention it to your vet at your next visit. It happens to this breed. It's probably nothing."

"Thanks."

As they neared the exit, Feingold stopped to shake his hand again. More formal now, the send-off shake, a left hand resolutely at her side this time, already having completed its commando task of reeling him in. Feingold presented him with her card in case there were issues, and as he turned to go, he could already imagine her returning to her office to note this in the chart.

Brendan drove north on Highway 15, through what seemed to be the deepest part of early-summer Vermont, the forest's canopy strobing blue sky above him in a car-commercial way that occasionally happened in life. Everything along the road was lush, almost a little luridly so, and stood in stark contrast to the suede valleys and snow-hooded hills that had greeted him on arrival a little more than three months before.

The improvement in Martin's condition during that time had been startling—even that morning, Brendan had arrived at his brother's room, to find him casually reading a Dunes pamphlet about fall prevention—and listening to Feingold talk about his eventual departure should have been a culmination. Instead, Brendan was already fighting the swells of anxiety about what would happen next. Getting Martin home, figuring out how to get him fed and to his appointments, the details and the dailyness of Martin care. Then there was the delicate matter of explaining to Martin that he was no longer a partner in his firm. Brendan gently probed his brother with questions about what he recalled, but it was clear from the start of his recovery that Martin remembered nothing of the contract that severed ties with the firm he had founded.

Brendan had come across the buyout contract, signed by Martin and his partners a mere week before the crash, sitting on the kitchen table of Martin's Montreal condo on one of his first trips back there to deal with the legal issues. With this fact erased from his memory, Martin rose from his Dunes bed to give every appearance of wanting, of expecting, to walk through the doors of his now-former company, sit down to work, and start building again. Brendan witnessed firsthand how Martin's amnesia and eagerness to get back on the job stunned his partners that day they ventured down to the Dunes for a commiserating visit, the lady architect almost speechless and in tears and the other partner reduced to simply nodding and going along with Martin's rambling plan. Martin—misinterpreting their incomprehension as a simple vote of no confidence—seemed even more triumphant after they left, energized by what seemed to be the need to prove everyone wrong with a full recovery, to win back his life.

How do you deprive someone of that? Running on the fuel of false assumptions, Martin had begun reading again, was starting to muse about obscure Soviet architects, and was deep into making plans for a triumphant career return, albeit a return to one that had ceased to exist in the way it was imagined, but who was he to debunk his brother's hope? *Back in the tomb, buddy, it turns out you're actually just a dead carpenter.* Brendan had to admire the passion and admit, in a way, that he was more than a little jealous of his brother, recognizing the times in his life he could have profited from a little deluded therapeutic badassery himself. No, Martin Fallon was as happy as Feingold's Doberman, and Brendan decided he wasn't going to be the one who stopped either tail from wagging.

A half hour later, he was back in his suite of the hotel on the outskirts of Burlington, which had become his temporary home, with a view of Lake Champlain and a kitchenette, where he started to prepare an evening meal. Two years of widowhood had made him understand that the silences around a meal without Rita would be filled, one way or another, and that he might as well fill them with the effort to cook. One full, self-prepared meal, every day. This had been his goal, prompted by the suggestion of a psychologist he had seen, his own Feingold, and it had saved him. Brendan had found copies of Rita's recipes—the originals had been spirited away by his sons, taken out to Portland, where they now served as the foundational documents of La Cucina della Puccio, an Italian food truck they operated and had named in honor of their mother and her family—and he promised himself he would at least attempt a competent approximation of those tastes and textures. The effort of planning and the small, organized tasks of preparation calmed him, and over the course of the last year he had finally begun to experience success consistently. It was gratification at being able to preserve something of value. It was mastery of something that had eluded him and a tribute to the woman he loved. It was good food.

After dinner, once the dishes were done and he had found a Tigers game on television to drown out the other news, Brendan retrieved Feingold's card from his pocket. He imagined her response a couple of weeks hence when she found her dog dead. Fainting in a four-year old Doberman was a classic presentation of a heart ailment to which the breed was prone, one that would soon lead to sudden cardiac arrest and death. It was untreatable and unavoidable, and he'd explained the diagnosis, both before and after the terminal event, countless times to shocked and tearful owners. He didn't know if Feingold, when the time came, would recall his advice and curse him for what she would wrongly assume was either his ignorance or his willful deception. He hoped she might eventually understand that he was trying to give her a few weeks of unweighted companionship with the doomed animal. This was a gift, he thought as he looked out the window for that view of the eastern edges of Lake Champlain, although it was his experience that in the wake of loss, it was a gift rarely appreciated and never acknowledged.

Chapter 3

It was clear to Martin that Konstantin Melnikov had awakened him. It was difficult for Martin to remember anything of the Dunes before he had recalled that moment, that thrilling and distorted memory of wading through the weeds in front of Melnikov House with Professor Lanctot. He wondered how a memory just *arrived,* how one index card of a life was pulled from the roll. Or maybe it was simply random arrival, another effect of a million brain cells being tumbled together, and he was just as likely to have had a memory of a song that Susan or Norah sang or the taste of a spoonful of cornflakes.

However the memory came, whatever guided it, it was made more meaningful in the way his other thoughts began to array themselves around it, thoughts crystallizing into a thin layer of him. Perhaps, before all this happened, he was aware of being an architect, but he was not aware of the awareness until he stood at the north side of Melnikov House with Lanctot. *I am Martin Fallon.* What followed was a sequence of declarations, the reassertions of a person lying in a strange bed. He was unsure if he said any of it outloud.

I am Martin Fallon.

I am an architect.

I have been in an accident.

I have two daughters.

I would like this catheter taken out.

He became aware of day and night and then the subsidiary divisions of the day: the nursing shift, with its quickly decaying enthusiasms and own internal rhythms, then the biological satisfactions of meal arrival, and then finally the smaller, more urgent decrements of medication schedules. The swell and trough of narcotics. The effect like a choke chain on a dog. He was suddenly aware that he had preferences, for certain orderlies or nurses—was this a sign of a growing self-awareness? Pickiness? He became more argumentative with nurses, and not just the ones he didn't like. He started to fall, because, he argued, he was starting to walk. This was a good thing. The medical staff didn't see it that way.

It was shortly after he recalled the visit to Melnikov House that he began to remember details of the consulate project, the commission his firm had been involved with at the time of his accident, and this arrived with a sidecar of panic and frustration, as though something vital to the design still lay unrecovered. And while the specifics of this forgotten detail were achingly just beyond retrieval, for some reason he could easily remember Jean-Sebastien nervously teasing him anytime he obsessed about their consular clients—*Don't worry, Marty, they're only Russians. What're a bunch of Russians gonna do to us if we fuck up their consulate?*

Luckily, the anxieties did not arrive alone. He could feel, and then move, his left hand, a triumph occurring so suddenly that he was convinced it was effortless, the hours spent in physio transformed from a futile drudgery to a superfluous one. For a while, every day brought a change, clusters of new functions returning, new aptitudes reemerging, sleeper cells of forgotten skills responding to a mysterious call from afar. He could walk. His energy returned. There was an odd, appealing velocity to all of it. His appetite returned. He could remember who had just spoken to him.

He began to venture out of his room, edging along the Dunes's corridors first in a wheelchair, then in a walker, always getting stuck in a certain cul-de-sac, where Szandor invariably found him, saying, *Here's our Mr. Right Turn* as they headed into the mysteries of the trip back to his room.

It was in that room at the Dunes that he realized what exactly had changed about him. As Szandor turned off the light, he became aware of the arms that lay on either side of him, how they felt connected to him now. He closed his eyes to make the darkness more complete, and this was rewarded with an enhanced awareness of the bed around him, a finer, more discriminating sense of the bed as a plane on which he lay. Each hand slowly crab-walked away from his body to the edge, wrists touching the cool chrome of the bed rail. His fingers flexed and he knew where he was, that this was a bed, with its length and breadth; this was where he was, all of it coming to him with a certainty that was absent with the lights on and his eyes open.

He forced himself to stay awake, easier once he had pushed through the walled cotton of his evening dose of pain medication. His hands traced and retraced the contours of the bed linens, fingers brushing against ridges and seams. The scrubland terrain of a hospital bed. Registering all, reporting all. Martin turned back the sheet and crawled out of his bed with a newfound confidence in his ability, moving silently in the darkness. On all fours, his hands scouring the floor of his room, he moved with surprising authority until he had reached each floorboard and mapped out the territory completely. The bathroom was last, and it felt like a triumph of his senses, able to discern the miniature tiles and grout that hemmed them in. He put his face to the floor and breathed in, telling himself he could sense the slope that led to the center of the floor, running his thumbs over the little grille of the drain cover. Touch the sink, touch the toilet. It all made sense in the dark. The surfaces became real under his hands and the space at once inflated around him, assuming the dimensions of a small room. The room existed again, and this discovery—by necessity made with him on all fours, crouching close enough to the toilet that he could hear the muffled liquid hiss of the water-works underneath the porcelain skin—made him feel a gratitude so tender that for a moment he felt able to forgive all the indignities he'd been made to endure. In one revelatory moment in the bathroom, he felt certain not only that he had recovered but that he had been granted a quite remarkable experience. A gift. He knelt and wiped his hands of Dunes dust, Dunes dirt.

This continued for weeks. Every evening, once the night shift had retreated to its garrison of the nurses' station and the hallway lights were turned down, he would begin the sortie around his room. With increasing ease and a stealth he took pride in, he would reclaim a little more of the Dunes territory for himself each night. And when a particularly ignorant orderly left the light on in his room—a past-due fluorescent that hissed a spray of cold light—it offered him the chance to discover that the light—or darkness—meant nothing, that simply closing his eyes was sufficient to escape into a world of spatial awareness.

He could have told Feingold about this, about his new appreciation of space, but he suspected that she would regard this as a curiosity. To reintegrate into the world, he suspected she would say, the last thing that he needed to do was to close his eyes. She'd told him he had become well enough to be a danger to himself, stranded in that gray area of recovery that nobody talks about, a trajectory leveling off. The birth of a plateau. And a plateau is nowhere at all.

And along with all the declarations of who he was, and what he'd been, really, there came what he recognized as some internal engine starting again, an engagement, vague but palpable. Even if he could not immediately understand it, it gave him pleasure, because it felt like appetite. Sitting there listening to Feingold, helpful, useless Feingold, he understood what this appetite was for.

He didn't tell Feingold about Melnikov, or the architect's role in his awakening. This was a good sign, he thought, asserting the need to have a secret as a sign of burgeoning autonomy. Besides, he thought, if Feingold knew, chances were that she would claim Melnikov's appearance as her own therapeutic victory, as her patient's first step to creating the linear that she had suggested. He picked up the digital recorder she had left for him and massaged the RECORD button and had a brief conversation with his own voice.

I am Martin Fallon. Each sentence the laying down of tracks of a personality. *I am fifty-six years old. I live in Montreal. I am an architect. I have two daughters.* He listened to the voice talk about itself, the echoes of a newly born ghost, and it made him grimace. He ran the message back, stopped, and waited.

Chapter 4

It was surprisingly easy to escape the Dunes.

He had been there long enough that he could imagine the aftermath of going AWOL, how the staff would establish an "estimated time of disappearance" after they couldn't find him during the morning medication rounds (the chronic care trifecta of narcotic, anti-inflammatory, and laxatives that he'd begun to wean himself off). Or maybe they would notice he was gone when he didn't show for lunch. People had gone missing before, he was told, wandered away in the spring sunshine or just lost track of time. Lots of Dunes clients were like that. Often it would take nothing more than announcing the missing person's name over the PA system to rein them in. If there was still no answer—a rare event in his weeks at the Dunes—a search would commence, with pairs of staff going from room to room until the wayward client was located. He tried to imagine the sound of his name on the PA system, echoing in the hallways. But he could not remind himself of the sound of an echo. There was just sound and then less sound and then silence.

He doubted they would spend much time calling out his name or doing the door-to-door search. They'd have the good sense to check the logbook to find out that Brendan was his last visitor. Having his brother sign him out gave them a grace period of a few hours more. Maybe they would just change the linens and the name over bed 412-C and wouldn't bother to chase after him at all.

It was AWOL, though, and that thought made him smile. Not a difference of opinions, not a discharge against medical advice. He was gone. He'd walked out, a statement in itself to Feingold and the rest of the Dunes rehab-industrial complex.

Brendan hadn't initially agreed with his decision to leave the Dunes. He repeatedly mentioned the caliber of rehab at the Dunes and more openly questioned Martin's judgment, asking several times for Martin to sleep on it, raising suspicions in Martin that Brendan was going behind his back to Feingold. Over the course of several visits and endless phone conversations, Martin pleaded his case to Brendan; the humiliation that he might have felt was muted by a pleasant nostalgic pang—that almost-forgotten desire to edge into a world of increasing freedom and danger that was cordoned off by an elder brother. He knew better than to appeal to his brother's sense of duty and switched to a pragmatic approach. He had recovered, he told Brendan. *Can't you see that?* And while he was grateful for all that Brendan had done, for Feingold and the OTs and the physios who walked him until he no longer staggered like a zombie, he was ready to leave. That was the goal, wasn't it?

Even after this, Brendan hesitated, perhaps understanding that for any escape he would have to be his brother's necessary accomplice, beginning to realize that this was a commitment not simply to escort Martin out of the Dunes but to do something potentially more difficult and open-ended. But to the surprise of them both, Brendan did not flinch, even when he got past the notion of aiding and abetting escape. It was Brendan who volunteered to go up to Montreal to help Martin get settled, to pilot the disability-insurance paperwork through proper channels and hold the fort until they could hire someone to stay with him on a more permanent basis.

They are brothers, Martin overheard one occupational therapist casually mention to another to explain Brendan's presence. At the

Dunes, simple phrases like that were weighted to the point of being foundational truths, conveying meaning as effectively as they suppressed all other meanings. A brother at the bedside trumped all other subsidiary stories, and so all were spared the explanation of the almost thirty-year estrangement, their relationship ruptured by a war that sent Martin to Canada and his elder brother off to Southeast Asia. There are things that social workers never know, and probably shouldn't care about. Simple, uncontested presence is enough. And so Brendan's role was accepted with no more explanation than having his parking validated.

Brendan had been the one constant during his recovery, the unexpected presence as he slowly pieced himself back together at the Dunes. His brother even rented a house an hour from Burlington, so much the better to visit the Dunes daily, and, along with Melnikov, he became a compass point in those early, otherwise-fragmented days (for a brief period, Martin thought that Brendan was the architect himself, sitting down to tea and a conversation). There was also a briefer moment of conflation, when he had confused Brendan with his mentor, Lanctot. Then Brendan's presence finally merged with the idea of his brother, when his voice became his own at the bedside. Brendan was the man who would be there waiting in Martin's room when he returned from his morning physiotherapy session. They would spend the first half hour talking, which more often than not involved Brendan just listening and then trying to calm his brother's fleeting, minor-key obsessions—he assured Martin no one was stealing from him and reassured him that the noises outside his window that greeted him each morning were nothing more ominous than birdsong. Later, usually after a lunch taken in his room or in the large fourth-floor common area, the two men would gravitate to the veranda of the Dunes for an afternoon of sunshine and therapeutic silence, taking their places among the other clients wrapped in thick blankets against the breezes that swooped down from the Green Mountains.

There was no talk between them—which felt oddly natural and logical for brothers who had shared their early years in the same twelve-by-sixteeen-foot bedroom in Highland Park. Brendan never explained why he would simply appear in his brother's life. And Martin never asked, instead choosing to pass the time tilting his head at the gently buckling vista of mountain foliage and schist. There was no talk of family between them as they sat on the veranda with the other wheelchaired and stretchered inhabitants of the Dunes. No reminiscences or hearty reunion chatter, no small talk even, all of which was an enormous relief to Martin. They were brothers; that was all they needed to know. This was their default bond, and the dividend was not having to explain anything to anyone. In truth, no explanation was necessary, at least to others; fellow clients' families and staff freely commented on the similarity of their looks: hair the color of steel wool retreating in identical patterns, bricklayer-thick hands they inherited from their father and were forever trying to hide in pockets, a jaw that cantilevered prominently enough that it gave the impression of being set against some fresh insult.

It fell to Brendan to explain, over and over, what had happened to Martin. The details of how Martin had gotten to the Dunes, a montage of images and sensations assembled into something that seemed real enough to pass for memory. The early hours of a February morning. A highway hidden under snow and through it all, through the darkness and the whiteness, the blade of a snowplow scything toward him, pointing him toward the Dunes. The collision—predictably high-velocity, high-impact—launched him into the darkness and ditches that straddled Highway 108 in the Eastern Townships of Quebec.

He must have been going up to the cottage in the Townships. He had no recollection of the journey, and it made little sense for him to have gone to the cottage in February. He was found by the local police. Oddly, he could visualize this part very clearly: Countless trips up to the cottage had been slowed by detours around accident scenes—images of roadside flares, yellow tape, and siren wail pounced on him, as well as a Sûreté officer scrambling down the slopes of the ditch. Of course, all this was a reconstructed midsummer scene, not occurring, as it had in reality, in the dark heart of February. A rescue crew extricated him from the crumpled accordion version of his BMW. Emergency neurosurgery followed, this fact ably confirmed by Martin's own right hand searching through the stubble of his hair to find the smooth worm of a scar punctuated at each end by an indentation that he learned were burr holes. Fractures of both legs and his pelvis. (Just the mention of this injury made Martin wince, but in truth a fractured pelvis sounded far worse than he remembered its having felt). Four weeks of coma, another six weeks on the traumatic brain injury unit at Hôpital Sacre-Coeur passed before he was transferred to the Dunes. Later, Brendan admitted the circumstances around having him transferred, that he'd contacted both of Martin's ex-wives—Agnetha back in Montreal and Sharon, predictably, engaged in something heroic in some village near Khartoum—for permission to transfer him to the Dunes, choosing to save his younger brother from the potential indignity of knowing that he had faced no opposition whatsoever from either woman in taking charge of Martin Fallon.

And for a time, while Martin was emerging from the haze of those first weeks at the Dunes, Brendan's voice was indistinguishable from his own, his brother's words providing the moment-by-moment narrative of who he was and why he was there. At some point, Martin had regained this ability for himself, a seamless transition, acknowledged only in retrospect. Suddenly, he had his own voice again, his own thoughts and desires. It was as though he had taken control of the wheel that had momentarily been in the hands of another.

Martin steadied himself as they pulled out of the Dunes parking lot, his brother's car already cradling him in a series of gentle luxury-sedan tugs, micro g-forces of push and pull, all mediated through the most extraordinary seats with calf leather the color of a suntan that God would have longed for. Had he not known that Brendan was this wealthy, he would have wondered again how a veterinarian could afford a car like this, much less the tab for a couple of months at the Dunes. Perhaps he'd been pet-free for too long—the last a poodle-something mix they'd had when Susan and Norah were children. Back then, vets seemed happy to aspire to that hippie/Saint Francis of Assisi persona that made him forever associate a professional interest in animal welfare with a vow of poverty. But then again, Sharon was always the one to take the dog to the vet.

Martin tried to sit forward, but the seat belt engaged and restrained him. He looked outside and followed the world rapidly becoming a blur, shapes disorganizing into tumbling, indecipherable arrays of roadside color, relieved only once they reached the constancies of scorched earth that always borders interstates. Then Brendan said something, and the sounds of words startled Martin. It surprised him that anyone else was beside him, and he thought at first he must have believed he had awakened in his room, that he was still at the Dunes. Yes, it was the car, the simple unfamiliarity of the car. He wanted to say something to Brendan, just to hear the voice again, falling on him like it came from the Dunes PA system, some understandable sound to remind him he wasn't alone.

They drove north on the 89 out of Burlington. It was a route Martin had taken many times before, but now the surroundings streamed by in an unfamiliar way, broken down into source colors of green and brown and gray. The journey to Montreal, as Brendan explained it, was straightforward. Drive north on the 89, take the bridge over Lake Champlain into the most northeast corner of New York State before crossing into Quebec. Then a straight run north to Montreal. Martin's right hand explored the area of the car door, running fingers over upholstery, brushing up against the knobs and buttons before burrowing into the side pocket of the door and retrieving a map whose folds immediately sprang open. This was his brother, he realized, even with a GPS and a simple trip, he was always the one with a plan B. But a map—now recoiling in his hands like an accordion—he hadn't used a map for travel in years. Martin put his face close to the paper and smelled it, then put a finger and thumb on either side of the folds and pinched it tight. He understood that he still needed the feel of paper, and took what he knew was an inordinate pleasure in sharpness of folds of a freshly bought map. There was a pang for the way a blueprint placed upon a table would reveal itself under his spreading hands. He tried to read the map but could not find a way out of Vermont. What he could distinguish were lines of red marker that had defaced the map, marking intervals. Martin guessed these marks must be prospective rest stops—pee breaks—and it angered him, made him feel like someone enfeebled, that his escape wasn't an audacious prison break at all, but a process that required planning and considered effort on Brendan's part. Leaving the Dunes was a staged ascent, he thought, and getting him home was like hauling a dilettante climber up Everest. He was a man who needed Sherpa care and good weather and the permission of his brother.

"Do you have a cell phone?" Martin asked.

"Whom do you need to call?"

"I asked you if you had a phone. It's a yes or no question."

"Whom do you need to call?"

"Susan."

"Look, I'll be with you. You don't have to call Susan."

"No, it's about work."

"Work can wait."

"Could you please just give me your phone? Please?"

Brendan squirmed in his seat and produced a phone and handed it to Martin, who spent a good minute with it before returning it, asking him to dial Susan's work number. He followed Martin's directions and waited. Then Brendan held the phone to his chest.

"I've got her voice mail. Do you want to leave her a message?"

"No. Forget it. I need to speak to her in person."

Several weeks before, Martin had been visited by his two partners—they'd made the trip down from Montreal to spend an awkward half hour that had had all the personal engagement of a royal visit to the outer colonies; flourish of arrival, distanced chitchat, a smile and a hope that it could all be put behind them with a departing wave. As he lay in bed that night, Martin could imagine Jean-Sebastien and Catherine leaving, too excited to talk as they made their way back to the parking lot, trying not to break into a run as they contemplated the redistricting of authority and resources. The fact that his daughter Susan was a recently hired associate in the firm wasn't an obstacle to a coup they were obviously planning. When it came to administrative maneuverings, associates like Susan were little more than pylons. And apparently, Susan hadn't done anything to challenge his view of office politics. All that was left was the shuffling of names on the business cards and letterhead. But imagining the glee that must have been shared between them as they drove back to Montreal had infuriated him, made him want to ask Feingold if a person could rehab out of pure spite. Yes, he should have been the one to send flowers to Jean-Sebastien and Catherine. Seeing them was the alarm bell that he needed, a reassertion of the connection to his life that the pastorale of the Dunes had almost severed.

Martin suspected neither Jean-Sebastien nor Catherine was prepared for how far he'd progressed. Yes, he thought, that's what made them uneasy during the visit. They'd written him off and then found him awkwardly alive, a fish still wriggling on the floor of their boat, still something they'd have to contend with. He wanted to tell them that he was going to return to the office sooner rather than later, and that he expected to be briefed on ongoing projects.

And then there was the consulate. He wanted to ask them about the consulate. It was an urge, oddly translated into a deep, seemingly abdominal ache with a small spasm of panic, which up to that moment he had associated with hunger or the need to use the toilet. The consulate. He could not picture the small plaza that fronted it or any of the details of the north elevation; his memory of it was incomplete, and at some point in their conversation Martin felt the fingers of his hands extend involuntarily, a gesture that Catherine noticed, a gesture that was mysterious to him until he realized he was reaching out for the model, for the form of the building in another sense. He refrained from asking them about the consulate.

And so he asked about Susan: Why wasn't she down here? This caught Jean-Sebastien and Catherine off guard and drew a collective, almost principled silence (he could understand the pause from Jean-Sebastien, who even as a senior partner was prone to paroxysms of muteness and flop sweat anytime a presentation got derailed by a left-field query from a client, but Catherine,

Catherine was always so good on her feet, able to bob and weave out of the stickiest situations).

Catherine spoke first, God love her—he imagined the drops of perspiration trailblazing down the slopes of Jean-Sebastien's forehead at the mere thought of response—and said that Susan was swamped at the office, that he should be proud of his daughter, for even if she was still only an associate, she was keeping the Fallon name front and center in his absence. Besides, Catherine said, Susan visited weeks ago—a fact Martin couldn't dispute, a visit he convinced himself he could faintly recall, along with the other flashes from the Paleozoic era of his recovery.

He listened to Catherine, appreciating her reassurances until he realized that now *he* was the asshole client, sensing the tug of being led by the hand back behind the roped-off area of situationally appropriate questioning. The mammoth fruit basket that Jean-Sebastien and Catherine brought him sat on the windowsill, and in the lull of conversation their attention seemed to focus on that, the cellophane rippling in the reflected sunlight, as if a welder's torch lay hidden there among the fruit, shards and spokes of light drawing his eyes down into a squint.

It grew in him there. The germ of irritation, fostered and fed. He wasn't a client. He was their partner. They owed him more than evasiveness, more than a visit and a basket of fruit.

He asked what project Susan was working on, and Jean-Sebastien surprised him by taking over, each response a nonanswer about wanting her to get exposed to a variety of projects, giving her latitude to develop something about whatever. He smiled and tried to find Jean-Sebastien again, this time a different Jean-Sebastien, surprisingly confident, almost impudent, needing only the leveling effects of brain trauma for it to be a fair fight.

Tell me about the consulate, he wanted to say. How had

Melnikov's house and the consulate occurred to him when he hadn't yet relearned how to walk or toilet himself or tie his own shoes? Amid the frustration and the growing sense of panic—*Had they lost the commission because he'd been injured? Were they trying to spare him the disappointment?*—he'd come to understand that memory was not random, that it must be at service to obsession, that it fed the truest needs of the animal. He wanted to stand up, to get out of the chair, but he didn't trust his legs. Catherine touched the fruit basket and it crackled back and the light showered off it as though she were arc-welding the window shut. He closed his eyes. He couldn't stand it any longer.

"Where does the consulate stand?"

"Everything's looking fine. Schedule, budget," Catherine replied. "Don't worry about any of that, Martin. It's all being taken care of."

"I need to go to the office."

"It's not a great time for you," Catherine said. He almost opened his eyes just to see her facial expression.

"I need to get back to work."

"You need to get better, buddy," Jean-Sebastien said.

I am better, he wanted to say. He felt something at that moment, something understandable only later, the feeling as enlivening as anger except that, even flat on his back, it made him feel unique and potent and full of righteous potential. In the car, a few weeks later, the only way he could describe it was that it felt majestic. He would prevail. Martin felt certain of it. But at the time, he said nothing to Catherine and Jean-Sebastien. It wasn't a conversation between equals. It never is when only one of the parties is wearing pajamas.

They crossed into New York State and then into Canada at Hemmingford, a smaller crossing to avoid the lines of semitrailers and the hydrocarbon fug of diesel smoke. Brendan showed both their papers and explained the situation to the Canadian border officials. Smiles all around. Service-industry banter. Martin listened closely and was thoroughly impressed. He reasoned that an American repatriating an invalid Canadian at the sort of backroads border crossing likely favored by traffickers of all stripes was enough to provoke a free-for-all interrogation (a strip search and a thorough snouting from their dope-sniffing beagle wouldn't be out of the question). But the guards simply waved them through. *You have a good day, too.* Brendan dealt with it effortlessly, completely at ease with these people he didn't know and wouldn't see again. This was not at all like his brother, not the Brendan Fallon he remembered, and for a moment Martin panicked at the fact he hadn't really *looked* at his brother, that he'd accepted this man for who he said he was, accepted the plausibilities of his brother simply appearing at his bedside, ready to care for him. The Brendan he remembered was not at ease with anyone, not with the counselors who saw him through the first difficult years after his return from Vietnam, not with their parents—in telephone conversations Martin's mother would only hint at the eruptions Brendan suffered after he got home, the drinking and the fallout of a precipitous marriage that failed before it saw a second anniversary.

Maybe his concept of Brendan had been fixed at a certain point, now only preserved under the intervening years of their estrangement. He'd half-expected him to show up at the Dunes in army fatigues. But of course Brendan had changed, and the changes seemed to be almost an insult to admit—not in its particulars but in a larger sense, that the world, so firmly entrenched, so richly registered, should have the nerve to reassert itself and demand reevaluation.

The banter at the border crossing shouldn't have surprised

him, he reasoned. Brendan had become a different man; with counseling and AA and maybe just time, he had turned his life around years ago. Their father had been the one to convince Brendan to go back to school on the GI Bill, and Brendan ended up spending four years at veterinary school in Madison—an ideal vocation in Martin's estimation: The simple moral mechanics of helping a blameless animal seemed to be ideal for someone who had been through Brendan's traumas.

With a monthly telephone call—always done with his father out of the house—Martin's mother kept him up-to-date on Brendan's progress, and yet this new life never fleshed itself out, so to speak, never seeming anything more than theoretical. The veterinary clinic Brendan started in Westchester prospered, acquiring a satellite and evolving into the more lucrative cosmology of a chain of clinics (at times, especially when his own career was stalled in gas station retrofittings and designing outdoor decks, Martin imagined Brendan's clinics as the rusty anchor of every wretched strip mall). While watching television coming from stations in New York State, Martin would occasionally see his brother's smiling face beaming back at him from advertisements for his clinics. Even then, watching the slick ads—smiling actors, lustrous dogs, and, he had to admit, well-designed clinic interiors—the scale of Brendan's success seemed separate from the man Martin had known. For him, his brother was forever cloistered at home, still skulking in fatigues, shaking a fist at imagined Vietcong somewhere in the darkness of their house.

Martin looked up and his head gave a mackerel jerk as a huge sign-size swath of highway green swooped past his right ear. The seat belt pulled tight across his chest and the world continued to twist and spin with an unsettling carnival quality. He pressed his eyes shut firmly against the light and tried to sleep, waking occasionally to reassure himself with the details of the inside of the car's passenger-side door. Music filled the car with the cultured jujitsu kicks of some anonymous philharmonic. It was a clearer version of the same sort of music that was forever playing in the Dunes, hosing down the place from morning to night, so pervasive and constant that he assumed the music must be some well-intentioned institutional policy; *good for their brains,* just like they recommended for babies, more likely to wire properly if exposed to industrial doses of Mozart. The music became inextricable from other aspects of the Dunes, from the labyrinth of corridors and verandas, specifications that he couldn't understand, dimensions like thirst. To Vivaldi, the clients would be brought out to sit in the sun with their blankets and feeding tubes and special chairs and watch the hills turn that lurid, almost fluorescent green when the trees budded in mid-April. Veranda time was 1:00 to 2:00 P.M., every day, during which he was treated to the spectacle of landscape in that corner of the Green Mountains and the inescapable companion music of the Baroque era. The scenery would carpet-fold and buckle in front of him, a frozen sea. He said nothing to Brendan, but it bothered him. Maybe it was the music.

Martin awoke some time later, alarmed, not knowing where he was, thinking he was somehow alone. Martin felt an arm reach across his chest and assumed it was Szandor, that he was waking up in his room in the Dunes.

"You okay?"

The sound shocked Martin. Not Szandor's voice at all. He reached up with his own right hand and felt the forearm, followed it toward its elbow, where it was pressed against his own.

"Where are we going?"

"I'm driving you home. We'll be there soon"

Martin's right hand settled into his jacket pocket, finding the digital recorder that Feingold had given to him. A parting gift. Maybe she'd known he would bolt. Of course she'd known. His thumb massaged the edge of the little machine, running over the controlling buttons like it would the backbone of a small animal. *Concentrate on the linear.*

"Testing, testing . . ."

"If my driving is what's making you think of dictating your will, I can slow down a bit."

"It's just a little exercise. Feingold's idea."

"Like one of those recovery journals?"

"Well, I suppose that was the point," Martin said. *Recovery journal.* Christ, a phrase that practically carried its own air quotes along with all the other carefully balanced baggage carts of self-congratulation and self-pity. It didn't help that Martin toggled a button on the recorder and was reminded of that small abyss between his recorded voice and how he imagined his voice sounded. His next thought was of opening the window and flinging the little machine and what was left of his voice into a convenient roadside ditch. What stopped him was the deep and undeniable yearning to say something and for that to be registered. To not be forgotten. To have his objections noted. To be heard, if only by himself.

"It could be therapeutic," Brendan said, and turned down the volume of the music.

The idea, when it came to Martin in the brand-new silence of the moving car, arrived so naturally, so specifically, that it were as though he had always had it but simply set it aside for later, for a moment such as this, where it was not only obvious but necessary. Now he knew: He would write about Melnikov. Not a monograph or an article, but just a story.

"I'm going to write about another architect."

"The Russian?"

"Yeah. Maybe."

Brendan said nothing more, which was just the endorsement Martin needed. And with that, he raised the recorder to his lips and, after sensing some form of machine life activate in the palm of his hand, felt relief to finally hear the familiar sound of his voice as it started on another man's story.

Chapter 5

"How long have you lived here?" Brendan asked as he struggled with the door, Martin leaning against a wall in a corridor he couldn't remember. Brendan finally mastered the lock and the smell hit them both, not the smell of him or anything personal, but the generic odor of an enclosed space being discovered.

"Last year. I moved here when Agnetha and I split up."

Martin found the couch and sat down. He watched Brendan walk by with a cardboard boxful of mail, some of it opened, and courier notification slips and small packages, tubes that even Brendan recognized contained blueprints. He set the box on the kitchen table and went to a window. With a grunt, he cracked the seal.

"Who opened my mail?"

"It was me. I got the keys from your super and just made sure everything was in order."

"Thanks."

"I'm glad you didn't have a dog."

"Turn on my computer."

"That can wait." Martin could hear the fridge door being opened. "You have any garbage bags?"

"Under the sink. I thought Susan would have dealt with some of this."

"Does someone clean for you?"

"I don't remember. I must've had somebody."

"I think you need somebody new."

"Maybe they thought I was dead."

Brendan said nothing. Martin heard a cupboard door snap shut and hoped Brendan had found a garbage bag, because he had no idea if he had any. Not a clue.

Hours passed. The better part of a day. It felt like a day from the couch. He would have wanted to get up and help, but fatigue from the day's travel had made it difficult not just to rise but to even change positions. Brendan disappeared and materialized throughout the day, padding around the apartment, accompanied by the sound of sustained housework, the effort required to reopen a cabin after a winter of abandonment. And while he was thankful for Brendan's efforts, there was something in his brother's industriousness that irritated Martin and caused him to groan more loudly than necessary as he tried to shift his position on the sofa. After chaperoning him to the bathroom (the door a respectful inch open, with Brendan listening for that unexpected silence that he had come to associate with Martin's imminent loss of balance and a toppling into the space between the bowl and the wall), Brendan declared he should go to the store for groceries for dinner. Before leaving, he checked several times with Martin about being left alone and was probably reassured, Martin thought, that not seeing Martin move independently in the previous two hours made risky, impetuous movements unlikely.

With his brother gone, Martin took off his sunglasses and tried to reorient himself in the condo. The main room hovered like a cloud forest around his head, all soft edges and puzzling depths, making it difficult to estimate where the bedroom was. The bathroom that he'd just visited seemed a profound mystery, as well. But that was to be expected, he thought; he hadn't lived here long enough for it to make an impression on him, occupying it for a scant six months after he and Agnetha split. Even signing for it, he'd recognized it was temporary. This was embarrassing for him to admit as an architect, but he hadn't cared about any of the condo's features except that it was available space when he needed nothing more. It was designed by another firm, Hattermas-Provencher, not a bad group, but gone a bit creatively fallow in the last five years, choosing to focus on the low-hanging fruit of loft conversions and never shy about contributing to off-island sprawl.

He ran his right hand along the surface of the sofa, flattening the folds in the leather upholstery into a more gentle terrain. This was where he lived. Big enough, close to work, a view of the eastern slope of Mount Royal (an extra, something that he wasn't looking for but which he remembered as an unexpected pleasure), and now as night fell and that view became a gathered plain of lights surrounding the void of mountainside darkness, he was convincing himself that the space felt familiar.

He closed his eyes and tried to rest but felt only a simmering of anxieties: work undone, plans left to the indifference of others, nothing that could be properly assuaged by lying on a couch. After months away, Martin now understood that he needed more than to simply reoccupy an address that happened to be his. He needed a higher form of physical assurance that this was home, and he understood immediately that it was the artifacts within the space that could grant that. The thought that he had papers and photos, books and mementos—the indisputable accrued sense of a life—that could be reclaimed reassured him almost as much as realizing that these things lay around him now.

He left the couch and crawled across the hardwood floor, tripodding along with one hand held ahead, reaching out in a continuous slow exploratory wave, occasionally making contact with an object, hesitating for a moment to estimate heft and dimension.

To calibrate space and identify. End table. Chair and standing lamp. Walls that marked the far end of the room.

This is your life, he told himself, something you get to wander through in darkness on your hands and knees.

He stopped when he came upon a stack of cardboard boxes in the corner of the living room, a little roadside shrine to the impermanence of this place. The reassurances of dry, flat cardboard surfaces bordered by rough edges. Orderly.

He convinced himself he could discern the faint ridges that hinted at corrugations underneath. His hands moved into the depths of the boxes—many left open, their flaps fluttering quietly under his hands like the wings of caged birds familiar with, and untroubled by, human touch. His thumb rippled up against the contents. Books. He paused on his haunches and suddenly the purposelessness of his actions disappeared. It was here, he thought, among the boxes.

Martin thought about turning on the lights, but it would be easier in the darkness. He knew it. The Styrofoam peanuts that spilled out of the freshly opened box confirmed he'd been right all along, and from there his hands became twin snouts, rooting down into the depths of the box until he could feel a balsa-wood edge. A few gentle tugs, each accompanied by another spume of tumbling Styrofoam, all of it reminding him of a Christmas morning as his daughters unwrapped something that they had so desired and that Sharon had known to buy and that was more a surprise to him than to anyone else in the room.

He finally extracted the balsa-wood model and placed it on the floor next to him. It was a model of Melnikov's pavilion in Paris, the quadrangle-shaped structure so familiar to him, bisected by a staircase that ascended to the center of the pavilion before descending to the opposite corner. Martin remembered having built it in the last year, as much to convince himself that he hadn't lost the skill—at the firm the task typically fell to a couple of competent junior associates or was subcontracted out.

Building the model had been deeply, surprisingly satisfying, and the result had pleased him so much that he had toyed with the idea of taking the model to the office. But he'd thought better of it. He didn't know why—perhaps, he thought, it was the hobbyist aspect of his desire to make the model in the first place—but he hadn't wanted Jean-Sebastien or Catherine to know about it. This reticence itself had nagged at him; he was the senior partner, the founding partner, and if he wanted to bring a damn model that he'd made into his office, there should have been no obstacle, real or imagined. He was owed this. He owed himself as much. Other architects had no such reservations about indulging themselves in this way or subjecting others to their eccentricities.

The public's conception of the most famous names in architecture was often attributable to nothing more than an assemblage of eccentricities—geodesic domes, the unlivable cities, the prototypes never built. But behind the extravagances, there was also the monomaniacal drive and vision and ultimately the beautiful remnants of that talent. It was clear to him that to be truly great, to be accepted as great, one needed that amalgam of style and substance. A catalog and a cultivated persona that allowed one to effortlessly add to that catalog. Once that happened, you were reborn as an adjective. This is a Wright house. *This is so Miesian.*

Fallon was not an adjective, he thought. He was pretty much like everybody else in the world of architecture: a noun. A noun that built other nouns. This state was the malaise of moderate, second-tier career accomplishment—and having the firm win a Governor General's award in architecture three years before only heightened the sense of a *ceiling.* He had experienced a taste that served only to tell him that a larger appetite remained. Unsatisfied.

It was a state of being that impelled him to listen for the winner of the Pritzker Prize to be announced, not with hope (even deluded) that it would be him, but with an appetite to formulating the most derisive and succinct critique of the winner should anyone care to ask his opinion. *Not the most courageous choice, but fine if deconstruction by numbers is to your taste.*

He came to realize that the antidote to everything—that perpetual sense of being thwarted, his increasingly apparent insecurities, and what he felt amounted to a paltriness of spirit—had been the consulate project. It was a commission that came along once in a career. It could take a firm to the next level. They could open a New York office. More than that, they would *need* a New York office. But the consulate needed to succeed. And for that, it needed him.

Martin touched the base of the model and then listened to the delicate zippering sound of his thumbnail as it ran up against the balsa-wood steps. He pressed the pads of his fingers against the walls of the pavilion, able to detect the details of the window frames. Martin's fingers extended and, with the delicacy of cat whiskers, sought out and made contact with the tower that rose from the north side of the building. He imagined the sound of hammering in that summer of 1925 in Paris, the wooden frame that the unknown architect was erecting. The walls of glass that captivated so many people.

He had been unable to come up with anything to say about Melnikov to the recorder Feingold had given him. The story of the architect's life was inside him, already written, but Martin felt unable to access it. Mute in the car, with Brendan listening, he'd simply cleared his throat and put the little machine away for the time when the words would come more easily.

He put the model aside and resumed his journey across the room, trying to recall where he was, reminded when he felt the reverberating thud as the heel of his hand met a pane of patio glass. He stood up, finally understanding the measure of darkness, finally feeling that he knew where he lived.

He was back on the couch when Brendan arrived with white plastic bags slung heavy with groceries. He listened but said nothing as the lights were turned on and the cupboards opened and closed and the food was put away. When Brendan was finished, he sat down in a chair opposite. His brother's face was not as familiar to Martin as it had seemed before. This was fatigue speaking, Martin told himself. This was what happened when you made the leap from Dunes to life. This was what happened when you left your plateau. This *is* Brendan, he told himself. He squinted and tried to enumerate the features that marked Brendan as a Fallon, but it felt like he was sitting with Feingold again, getting caught up in the shape of the details.

"You're awake." The voice helped. The voice was Brendan's. "Who made the mess?"

"Oh, that was me. Just getting my bearings."

Brendan nodded, apparently unfazed by the opened boxes and Styrofoam detritus. He was, after all, a vet, Martin thought, and coming home to a mess shouldn't have been an entirely new experience. Maybe he was even relieved it wasn't organic.

"You've got to take your medication."

"I don't need the painkillers."

"You have other ones you have to take." Brendan said.

Martin nodded but the thought of having to still take medication had eluded him. He associated the medication—the little plastic cups, the appalling variety of colors and sizes—strictly in the context of being at the Dunes; and now, like someone returned home from Africa, he assumed he could stop taking his malaria pills.

Brendan brought out a small plastic case with the multiple compartments each capped by tiny lids and placed it on the coffee table between them. If he concentrated, Martin could make out a container with small sealed compartments. A little pill mausoleum. Brendan pried one open one of the crypts and tilted the contents into Martin's hand.

"This is Dilantin." Brendan poked the pills in his palm with his index finger. He picked one up, examining it. It was a capsule, indistinguishable from the others.

"Yeah, I think I've seen that one. What's it for?"

"Seizures."

"Jesus, I had seizures?"

"Right after your operation."

"But not anymore."

"Well, no."

"So I don't have to take it."

"The doctor I spoke to said you have to take it for at least a year."

"Do you use it? With animals?"

Brendan stared at him. "No. We have different medications."

"These are laxatives. I know these ones," Martin said, staring intently, positioning his head in front of the capsules in a way that reminded Brendan of a particularly canine form of fascination.

"Right."

Brendan studied the case and turned it over. The contents rattled inside. A week's worth, Martin thought, imagining a series of plastic cups, stretching out into his past and future.

"The names and doses are written on the other side. Pain meds, Tylenol and anti-inflammatories. Pantoloc, to protect your stomach. Norvasc, for high blood pressure." He looked up at Martin. "Well, that's something we have in common. Thanks, Dad. And this is Apo-Fluoxetine. An antidepressant."

"Great, great. Where did you get all this medication anyway?"

"From your doctors."

"You told them I was leaving?"

"How else do you think they'd give it to me?"

"They knew I was leaving?"

Brendan nodded, perplexed at his brother's unease. "You wanted to get out, Martin. I signed a form for you, saying you left against their advice. That's all. You're out. Isn't that what matters?"

Martin nodded in response and felt the gesture arrive naturally, moving his head in agreement as his brother had done, the expression of something deeper than remembrance, something genetic, as he gathered the pills in his hand and waited for Brendan to return with a glass of water. It was an act slower than simply nodding, a movement that Martin felt could be sustained indefinitely, even incorporated into his everyday routine of living outside the Dunes. Useful even for swallowing pills.

The bed was different. Its dimensions, the firmness of the mattress, the smell of the linens. Martin tried not to let nostalgia for the comfort of the Dunes creep into the room. But everything was different. The rhythms of the Dunes had fallen away, the intrusions and interruptions replaced by silence in the night. He gave up on sleep and resigned himself to being stranded for stretches of this first night, admitting to himself that freedom felt like barely suppressed panic.

From where he lay he could hear Brendan sleeping in the other room, the frequent movements and interrupted snores that attested to a person making do on an insufficiently large sofa. At times during the night, Martin wanted to wake him up, to talk or just to break the routine of raspy snarls and snorts his brother had lapsed into, but he never moved from his bed, choosing just to listen to the sound of him. There was a familiarity to this; he had always been the insomniac, his brother the deep sleeper. He was younger by fifteen months, but keenly aware, as only insomniacs are, of the feeling that he was in some way destined to be a sentry for those who slept so deeply under the same roof. The grave responsibility of being conscious when others were not. As a child, he had spent nights awake, cataloging the sounds: the house shifting and the snores of his father (another Fallon bequest, one that he hadn't evaded, as Agnetha or Sharon could attest to). In those nights in Detroit in the late fifties, he remembered cricket song and the ebbing sounds of traffic and the screech of cats mating in the backgarden darkness. The noises of night, all felt as an additional, secret awareness of the world, a privilege to a child awake in his room.

In the nearly forty years since he'd left Detroit, he had seen Brendan only twice prior to his brother's reappearance at the Dunes. For Martin, these dates stood memorialized like battlefield engagements in the otherwise-separate history of hermit nations. More ironically, for Martin, whose only recent dealings with religious establishments were to oversee their conversion to condos, both meetings took place in church.

The first: October 1975, an estrangement of seven years already, he spotted Brendan sidling into the last row of the chapel of St. Patrick's Basilica in Montreal as the first adenoidal strains of Wagner honked out of the organ and Sharon appeared at the end of the aisle on her father Henry's arm. Martin was embarrassed to admit that at this crucial moment, his full attention had been pulled away from Sharon and instead focused on his brother, funneled into the concentrated effort of trying to gauge something—a condensed history of seven years, a prevailing mood, a rationale for silence and animosity—from a glimpse of another person's facial features. There had been a moment—again, with Sharon coming down the aisle, the pressure to refocus on her now looming like a moral imperative—of possible eye contact with his brother.

But Brendan's head was already averted downward, a hand flashing across his brow as it made the sign of the cross, the sudden momentary disappearance as he genuflected, in Martin's estimation less a gesture of true piety and more the guerrilla tactics of a man trying to look inconspicuous among the other churchgoers. Martin then turned to look at his mother in the first row, to see if she had registered Brendan's arrival. (At least a glance at his mother was acceptable in the context, preferable to what seemed like random, wanton scanning of the crowd). She stood impassively, exhausted from several days of maintaining the composure required to stand there and explain that her absent husband was not deceased but "indisposed" or "unavailable" which was preferable to the more honest "disinclined to come." In the chaos outside the church after the service, it had been impossible to find Brendan. He never appeared for their reception.

Less than three years later, in July of 1978, it had been Martin's turn to appear unannounced at church, his first time back in the States since leaving a decade before, Jimmy Carter's freshly minted amnesty allowing him to cross the border safely for his father's funeral, the presidential decree coming into effect late enough that arrest for draft evasion had been the plausible excuse for not attempting a reconciliation with the old man in his hospital bed as he recovered from the operation and the first, fruitless attempt at chemo. Martin had dreaded the thought of the wordless bedside reunion: fraught, overloaded with accrued history, the weight of which would smother any authentic emotion. Added to that, Martin knew his father well enough to understand he would revile a meeting where he was at such a disadvantage. He knew that such a meeting was clearly a fraudulent, performative experience, a gesture to satisfy Brendan and his mother while ignoring the needs of the very people who had to live through it. Torturing both, desired by neither. When the Carter amnesty finally came into effect, he understood the burden of a convenient excuse had been removed, and he'd finally been forced to think about what he would say should his father want to see him. But his father did not ask him to come home, and so he stood his ground.

When the news of his father's death finally came, it was unexpected, following a couple of weeks where he'd seemed to rally. There was even talk of his father going home from the hospital for a few weeks, a scenario that Martin was able to envision as a more agreeable setting for a sit-down. But a blood clot changed that. From the calf to the lung, and that was it, in Martin's mind like a suicide bomber's laden truck, traveling quietly through the streets of the city it would soon transform. Middle of the day and his father just stopped. Found cold in the bathroom.

His promise to himself to maintain distance, all, he repeated to himself, out of respect for his father, collapsed under grief and guilt and the pressure of a harried return from exile. It is one long, choked drive to the border, traffic from Toronto to well past London, an acrid fog of diesel fumes as they sat on the Ambassador Bridge, Susan less than a year old, cradled in Sharon's arms. He tried to imagine the array of pauses and frowns that would greet him at U.S. Immigrations and Customs.

The trip to St. Clare of Assisi was the last step in a succession of triggered memories, making him realize how bound humans are to place, seeing the tree-lined streets of his neighborhood and high school and the lawn in front of the church. He got out of the car and sent Sharon, exhausted with travel and morning-sick with Norah, off to their hotel rather than face a hot church and the contagion of the congregation's mood.

"This has all hit your brother very hard," his mother said to him later, without any irony, as she held a cold cloth to Martin's face and pinched his nose in the rectory of the church. It was the only explanation she would offer and was what would have to stand as an apology for what Brendan had done after the funeral service. Martin had joined them in their pew during the service, where they sat wordless after a handshake (a small but magnanimous gesture on his part, Martin thought, but still more than anything Brendan had offered at his wedding). Brendan had given the eulogy, looking to Martin like a man unfit for the job, not because of a lack of eloquence or gravitas, but simply because it was evident that the task quite possibly might kill him. His face reddened and his voice heaved and shook and he seemed to approach the point of physical collapse, but he managed to compose himself. He continued, and this impressed Martin. Several times during the eulogy, Brendan looked over at their father's coffin, placed in the center aisle, near the front of the church. Martin found himself glancing at the casket, too—only later, in contemplation specific to younger brothers, wondering if this had been an act of emulation or competition.

Perhaps it was observing how his emotions had almost undone his brother, or that he'd been able to experience vicariously a grief deeper than anything he felt, but the church service had the odd effect of allaying much of Martin's guilt about not coming home earlier. Despite not seeing his father before he died, he understood that they'd had differences that were not resolvable. He would have liked his father to hold his granddaughter, to know in some human, tactile way that only babies can accomplish that some greater part of him would live on. But the church service seemed to absolve him, made him realize that he had no regrets for the decisions he'd made. If his father hadn't understood that, then he simply hadn't understood him, and with that Martin felt vindicated in having stayed away. His father would have respected that. As the service ended, he felt he was able to appreciate the man in a manner more dignified than keening. Martin looked around the church, full of family and friends. This was a life well lived. This was a much-loved man.

Martin passed a half hour at the back of the church greeting and reuniting with people he hadn't seen since leaving Detroit: cousins from Akron; Mr. Phelps, a friend from the VFW legion who had served with his father in the Ninth Army; even the odd acquaintance from their days in Highland Park. Not exactly the welcome of the prodigal son, but warm enough, enough to make him grin at the thought of any reconnection with this place, this past. No cracks about draft dodgers or veiled comparisons with the brother who had honored his notice to serve.

After the church emptied and Martin finished the surprisingly satisfying process of greeting/reuniting/commiserating with the other mourners, he walked into the rectory and the firm right hand of his brother. It was a jab, not characterized by much power or accuracy (his grazed right collarbone was as sore as his nose) but with a surprising electrical sting to it, followed by the swell and gush of his own blood down his chin, all coupled with Martin's delayed staggering away from his departing brother.

His mother, who would have been within her rights to have simply sat and wept, did neither. With her two sons disgracing her on the most difficult day of her life, she showed a composure that was one of the more impressive acts of emotional control Martin would ever witness. She would deny it was her nurse's training and claim simple Scots pragmatism, the Glaswegian in her declaring itself among all the wailing and hysterics and now the inevitable flare of male stupidity, simply saying that this needed to get sorted. And so she pinched a handkerchief against the nose of her younger son and joined him there, sitting on the rectory steps, until the bleeding stopped.

Susan was asleep on a foldout cot when he got to the hotel. Sharon dozed at the window, her head leaning against the air conditioner, the grilles having left the impression of horizontal lines across her forehead that looked like the empty staves of an unfinished musical score. And as much as she was shocked to see him—she later described him as wild-eyed, the smell of sweat and tears and blood lacking only the stink of alcohol to complete the typical miasma of the Saturday-night gladiators she stitched up in an evening shift in the emergency room—she was more surprised to hear him say that they should wake up Susan. They were going home to Montreal.

Their mother had been their intermediary, the person from whom Martin had found out that Brendan threw the punch in response to what he saw as his brother's utter lack of decorum, his apparent frivolity after the funeral Mass. Until their mother's memory problems diminished her, she had been the way that each brother maintained contact with the other's life: the children and jobs and divorces, and through it all there was nothing she could do to get either to drop their parallel, perfectly counterweighted grievances: the punch and the reason for the punch.

And now, after almost thirty years and without explanation, Brendan had reappeared. This was Martin's life now, his brother's presence just another detail he had awakened to, another fact he could not understand but would have to reconcile. A marriage, a funeral, a punch and no words. He listened to this man breathing, feet away. This stranger. My brother.

The sun is up, Martin Fallon thought, but when he opened his eyes, his room was indistinguishable from its appearance at midnight. He heard neither snoring nor any other sound to suggest that Brendan had awakened in the next room.

A clock radio rested in its sentinel spot on his bedside table—its display a jumble of buzzing red ingots of numerical time that he couldn't focus on. A simple-stemmed lamp kept it company. The floor was smooth, the give and texture of a finely finished pine, he thought as he edged away from the bed.

On the small desk he found the medication case that rattled with the promise of the coming day's pharmaceutical victories. Beside this was his watch, which he could not remember wearing, much less having taken off, and his wallet proudly pocketed yesterday for the first time in four months. By the end of the car ride home, it had felt like a bull had gored his right buttock.

He found more objects behind a folding door, clothes that smelled of closeting. Tendrils falling from a tie rack. He rediscovered his personal hierarchy of laundry (shirts according to context of wear: leisure, office, business, presentation; socks garrisoned away from the inexplicably elevated status of underwear). From the suitcase opened at the foot of his bed he removed the clothes he had worn at rehab, the sweat suits whose partnered items were now separated into individual pants and tops that had cycled independently through use and laundry and whose ever-changing permutations comprised the Dunes uniform. He put his nose into the rayon-polyester blend. Who had bought these and why had he not protested? These clothes smelled different. Human use. They smelled stained, of sweat and urine, odors that he hoped were still evident only because of less regular, or rigorous, laundering at the Dunes.

He spent an hour like this, scuttling around, waiting for Brendan to awaken, before he stumbled across the digital recorder that Feingold had given him. He held it loosely, as though gauging its heft and value, the binary considerations of use or disposal.

Chapter 6

There was a hum on the third floor of the architectural firm of St. Joseph/Houde. Martin heard the hum. He was certain he felt it as he sat in the St. Joseph/Houde conference room. He had arrived with Brendan, stopped for a moment on the front steps to study the new sign that had replaced F/S+H, and then entered, announcing to the receptionist that he had arrived for a meeting with Catherine and Jean-Sebastien. This surprised the secretary, whose face and voice were profound mysteries, until she came out from behind her desk, took him gently by the arm, and introduced herself as Elodie. This proximity triggered a memory, a sweet olfactory blush of recollection. Elodie. He knew Elodie. She was whispering to him and he was leaning in and the easy intimacy of the moment—two voices hushed, the cadence of familiarity, the linked arms—along with the scent of her perfume made him wonder how he had ever forgotten her, made him long for a closeness that had systematically evaded him in five years with Agnetha. It was at the stairs that he realized Elodie was not leading him to the partners' offices, but to the conference room, where she sat him down on a chair. Brendan followed, perhaps too bemused to say anything, and joined him at the big conference table.

He heard scurrying along the bleached pine floors, the sound of activity in cubicles, Elodie no doubt alerting the in-house staff that the founding partner had turned up without warning, briefing them on how and where she had quarantined him. People arrived at the doorway, shadows that merged in the mid-morning glare, paying respects and then drifting away. Perfunctory, curious. If he had intended his arrival to be Napoleonic, his welcome told him this was Elba.

Fifteen years before, F/S+H had bought and gutted a four-story apartment block on avenue de l'Esplanade, just past rue Bernard, rented the bottom floor, and kept the top three for their grand reinvention. He and Catherine understood the move was a risk, not because it was pricey—back then Mile End real estate prices reflected the fact that the neighborhood was not yet a place that people wanted to stay in, much less seek out—but because Montreal was in a free fall, in the midst of a recession, stumbling toward another sovereignty referendum. The question was not whether to build, but whether to stay. Once the first question was answered, the second came painlessly. Together, they oversaw the conversion: Walls were knocked down to make a workspace; a staircase opened up to create an inner atrium.

Business doubled, with the new digs featuring prominently in their revamped image, becoming their best advertisement. Jean-Sebastien, then the newest partner, the visionary fresh from a year in Rotterdam, was given free rein to design a rooftop extension, and came up with a plan for a boardroom with a south and east wall of tempered glass to capture a view of the domain they had begun to conquer and what lay before them.

Jean-Sebastien produced a gleaming chamber (stunning, even he and Catherine had to admit). But because the adjoined panels of glass acted like a prism, catching and magnifying the sunlight during a critical period in the path of the sun, it produced a moving microclimate, a well-circumscribed "path" of extraordinary heat in the room for fifteen minutes every morning from April to

June. The heat would be upon its victim without warning, making that person feel like an ant twitching under the focused rays of the sun. Two feet away, another person would be fine, left to wonder why their neighbor was suddenly sweating and in such distress. Catherine was the first to recognize the phenomenon and refused to attend morning meetings in the boardroom during those months, citing partner privilege. Martin declined to sign off on changes in ventilation that might have remediated the boardroom "microclimate" situation, just as he vetoed an addition of louvers that would have cut down on the direct sunlight that caused such episodic and reproducible discomfort. This was to be a lesson for Jean-Sebastien, a flaw he was responsible for and one that he would have to continually acknowledge. Hubris, the unaccounted-for variables. Maybe he should have learned that in Rotterdam. Martin himself had forgotten all this, the confluence of place and time in this particular room, but the sun's rays reminded him. He put the cuff of his sleeve to his forehead.

From somewhere behind him, Jean-Sebastien appeared, shooing away some of the associates who had come to wish Martin well and inquire about the accident. The door closed. Not a word from Brendan, but Martin could still hear him, feel the reassurance of the odds somehow seeming to be made more even by family just sitting there.

"Jean-Sebastien, this is my brother, Brendan."

"Jean-Sebastien Houde. Oh yes, the veterinarian. I never knew you had a brother until we met in Vermont"

"Hmmph," came a mutter from Brendan's direction.

"So, hey, this is a surprise. It's wonderful to have you here. The place is buzzing, just seeing you, walking in on your own steam. It's great."

"Where's Catherine?" Martin asked.

"She's not in the office at the moment."

"Where is she?"

"I don't keep her hours, Martin."

"I would have liked her to be here."

"Then you should have given us some warning." A pause, Martin thought, just to let everyone get more uncomfortable. "The truth is that she can't bear this, Marty. She can't bear to see you like this. Now, what can I help you with?"

"I just wanted to know why," Martin said.

More silence from Jean-Sebastien. The acoustics were good in the boardroom, and the silences were emphatic, like in a symphony hall or at the bottom of a well. Martin listened to Jean-Sebastien breathe and was certain he could hear the remnant of a chest cold his partner had had as a child.

"I'm sorry, Marty, but I don't understand."

"I get home—after all that's happened, after months of trying to get better, after you and Catherine visited me, I finally get home and I find *this.*" From a breast pocket Martin pulled the lawyers' covering letter that fronted the buyout agreement that Brendan had walked him through earlier in the day. Brendan—familiar with the terms of just such a deal from his own business—had taken most of the morning pouring over and then highlighting the details of the deal, using a voice measured to be optimistically impressed yet not patronizing, gently emphasizing and reemphasizing what appeared to be the generous terms granted to his brother, only to look up and see an expression of pallid mortification on his brother's face. The only fact that resonated with Martin was that he was no longer a part of the firm he had created.

Martin unfolded the letter now, using both hands to spread it flat on the large conference table with the deliberateness of a man intending to consult an unfamiliar maritime map prior to some serious navigating.

"You're kidding, right?" Jean-Sebastien said, and shifted his gaze to Brendan, incredulous.

"He doesn't remember signing it," Brendan added softly.

"Martin," Jean-Sebastien continued as his former partner struggled with the letter in front of him. "*Martin,* this is what we all agreed to. Look at the last page. Everyone signed. That's your signature."

Martin's gaze seemed to sweep over the page. He turned away from Jean-Sebastien and slid his right hand along the table, running it over a second letter, which remained folded. Brendan knew it bore the crest of the Ordre des architects du Québec. At Martin's condo Brendan had read it to himself silently, and then to his brother. Two sentences informing Martin Fallon that, for medical reasons, his license to practice architecture had been suspended indefinitely.

"I spoke to the Ordre this morning," Martin said. His left hand trembled a little as it kept the letter flat in front of him. "I know everything. You asked them to revoke my license."

"I didn't ask them to do anything. We had to inform them about your injury. The restructuring deal hadn't taken effect and you were still technically a partner. It was necessary."

"*Jay-Ess.* Necessary? This is my life."

Jean-Sebastien nodded, looking from Martin to Brendan and back again. "There were obvious liability issues here after your accident, Martin. You . . . we have to face facts. You couldn't be an architect associated with the firm, even temporarily, with the impairment you have. I spoke to your doctors—" Martin opened his mouth, truly uncertain if a snarl or a muttered profanity would emerge. His objection was wordless."—your doctors, who don't feel you'll *ever* come back. I don't believe that. I'm in your corner. But this had to be done."

"I brought you in, Jean-Sebastien. I still want to be involved in the project."

"Martin, you signed an agreement," Jean-Sebastien's voice rose.

"Then bring me in as a consultant."

"To work on a design that wasn't yours? One that you said you could never stand to see built? You may not remember what you said, but everyone else in this office remembers." Jean-Sebastien looked around the room, as if the empty spaces would help him garner support. "Martin, listen to yourself. Even if we were to make you a consultant, even if the Ordre hadn't suspended you, with your problem, if you were to even appear anywhere near the project, the firm becomes the default shit magnet. Any problem, structural will point to us, construction will point to us, every subcontractor . . ."

"That's nonsense—"

"The public will go nuts. And that's not even talking about the Russians. You want the Russians suing you? You'd better hope they're only *suing* you." Jean-Sebastien looked around the room. "Projects go forward, Martin. You taught me that. Sometimes with us, sometimes without." Martin felt a hand on his forearm and had to fight the urge to throw off what felt like a gesture of bullshit bonhomie. "After I spoke with that psychologist . . ."

"You spoke with Feingold, too?"

"Of course. I had to." J-S paused. "Have you been doing any sketching?"

"Oh, enough with the condescension."

"It could help."

"Did Feingold say that?"

"I just thought—"

"Sketching. I'm not interested in 'sketching.'"

"You should take some time, for yourself."

"I understand things more fully than 'sketching.'"

"Sketching, drawing, whatever. Get the juices flowing."

"My juices flow differently now," he said, mumbling, looking for Brendan.

As he said this, Elodie appeared, materializing almost in front of him, carrying a tray that supported a pitcher of water and drinking glasses. She placed the tray on the large boardroom table, like a chessboard between them. Her hair was different, the light of the boardroom making it seem more blond. She had already turned to leave when Martin finally registered her perfume. An after-smell of vanilla that he hadn't noticed earlier. Subtle, a pleasant diversion for anyone who would have to share a seat with her on the Metro home that evening. He inhaled again; it was a relief to smell Elodie, another sense corroborating her arrival in the room. Maybe she had put on perfume for him.

"Thanks," Jean-Sebastien said as the glass door of the boardroom closed behind Elodie. "I got in touch with someone who could be interested in the magazine pieces you've written. The piece about Mies. And the Matta-Clark essay. You were talking about Melnikov; you were working on something about the house. Maybe you could put it all together in book form."

Martin shook his head. "I know busywork when I hear it. This is Feingold talking."

"Look at it however you want to. I'm just saying that I think you're not finished. But I think we have to be realistic. Everyone's happy to see you back, Marty; it's just that we have to accomplish a job within certain reference points."

"You were expecting me to come back. That's why you went to the Ordre."

"Marty, maybe one day you'll understand how much I wanted to protect you."

"I want to see my old office."

"I'm afraid I can't allow you to do that."

Martin wondered how Jean-Sebastien managed to get this way, how he'd been able to somehow inflate with the situation. People had specifications, just like buildings, and when it came to moments of pressure, to moments of confrontation, J-S was, in many ways, reliably not up to code. Everything had changed since that visit at the Dunes, two personalities retrofitted. It was as if everything he'd lost had been subsumed into the new Jean-Sebastien.

Martin nodded. "Then could I have a few moments alone here?"

"Sure."

The door closed and whatever hum that had existed before ebbed further into background noise, hiding in the ventilation ducts.

"Let's go," Martin said to Brendan.

Brendan stood and offered his hand, and his brother reached for it, balancing with the cane and hobbling to the door. At the bottom of the stairs that led from the boardroom, Martin pulled his brother sharply to the right, meeting with resistance.

"It's this way," Brendan said, correcting him.

"I know where I'm going," Martin replied, "trust me."

Together the two of them staggered along the corridor that opened up into a common work space, filled with the spacious planes of drafting tables, interrupted by computer workstations and the odd right angle of cubicle wall. They moved slowly, Martin putting himself through the indignity of parading himself through his workplace after being told to leave. He paused every few steps, a voice or a sound causing him to recalibrate. The fingers he didn't need to grip the cane were partially extended and brushed along the wall.

"Do you want me to describe where we are?" Brendan asked.

"I can see everything. I'm fine."

Martin stopped for a moment and turned to the right, edging down a small subsidiary hallway past a copier to bring them both to a doorway. With the tip of his cane, he pushed open the half-closed door, to reveal a small lunchroom. A woman looked up from her coffee, and except for a quick volley of estimation aimed at Brendan, she fixed her attention on Martin.

Martin smiled, "Hi, honey. I *thought* I heard you."

The woman put down her coffee cup; to Brendan, the expression on her face was disturbingly neutral. "Hi, Dad."

Chapter 7

The three of them stood in the lunchroom of St. Joseph/Houde and, for the acute embarrassment he felt, Brendan initially wished for nothing more than to turn and leave. What kept him there, he would later understand, was not an allegiance to Martin, but simple awe at being in the presence of a new, female Fallon. His first impression of his niece—and why hadn't their paths crossed at least once during his visits to Martin's apartment or during his stay at the Dunes, why had circumstance conspired against that?—was capsized by an unexpected swell of euphoria, the realization that the Fallons were capable of something beautiful and divergent, that there were permutations beyond the overlapping varieties of maleness in the two boys he'd raised. In the relative silence—a sleek little espresso machine hacked and burped in a corner—Brendan imagined a world of possible daughters, parallel families and experiences expanding and then collapsing into the moment again, with just the three of them and their definite histories. He studied Susan Fallon, trying not to squirm in her lunchroom seat under the vacant stare of her father, and as he did, Brendan felt an amalgam of pride and regret that he quickly attributed to a feeling projected onto his brother, a feeling that he reasoned must be the core emotion of having a grown daughter.

Brendan wanted to introduce himself, but he stood in silence, and she eyed him from time to time. Maybe she had seen pictures of him. Maybe Martin had established him in that way that the perpetually absent always seem to loom.

So he resorted to emoting, hoping his demeanor would help Susan understand that he was neutral here, but he felt like a cor-nerman for a staggering heavyweight, less neutral than simply pres-ent and ineffectual. He looked away as Martin reached out for the straight edge of a chair's back and pulled it out for himself. He groaned as he eased himself down.

"What are you doing here, Dad?"

"I'm feeling well, thank you for asking. I decided to come back to work."

"Is that okay with your doctors?"

"They're fine with it. I'm fine."

"I spoke with the psychologist—"

"Feingold. Yes, she spoke to everyone, apparently, a staggering breach of confidentiality, if you ask me."

"She wanted the best for you."

"Where's your mother?"

"She's still in the Sudan."

"Is that what she said, she said '*the* Sudan'?"

"That's just what people call it, Dad."

"It's always seemed like an affectation to me. *The* Sudan. Like people who say Nee-har-ah-wa."

"Well, maybe she didn't say 'the Sudan,' but she's there."

"Did she ask about me?"

"Of course she did. She and Eric were almost ready to come home right after the accident. If she wasn't in the middle of a proj-ect, she probably would have. She spoke to your brother. . . ."

Brendan held out his hand.

"I suppose I'll have to introduce us. I'm Brendan Fallon." Susan smiled for a moment, the novelty of new relations just another barrage that she wouldn't allow to unsettle her. She shook his hand, all the tensions of the moment paused for niceties. Then it was game on.

". . . and Mom knew that Brendan would be here."

"Lucky for her."

"So where's Agnetha in all this?"

Agnetha. It was a name that Brendan was coming to understand would be spoken of in a tone of matter-of-fact neutrality reserved for long-dead peacetime presidents. Acknowledgment of an office held without any emotion left over.

"Agnetha is far away, too. Farther than any Sudan, if that's possible. Just as well." Martin raised one hand and it flicked the air beside his head, as if shooing away a buzzing insect.

"And how are you feeling?"

"Perfect. A little unsteady on my feet. I have a lot of hardware in my legs now, so that's to be expected. Did they tell you that they had my license revoked?"

"I knew about it."

"No one told *me.*"

"No one expected you to just show up like this." With this, she looked at Brendan for a moment with what he felt was an indictment of his custodial responsibilities. She turned back to her father, who was now leaning in close over the table, whispering.

"I hired you, Susan. Do you know what I had to deal with to have you brought on here? Let's just say it was done over the strenuous objections of Jean-Sebastien and Catherine. I was your advocate."

"I've proven myself here."

"Of course, but you needed that initial chance. I gave you that chance."

"Dad, the Ordre des architects du Québec took away your license. Not me. I can't do anything about that."

"I could work as a consultant."

"I would lose my job for suggesting it."

"You owe me."

"Stop it."

Martin slid his hand across the table toward Susan. "This firm wouldn't exist without me."

With this, Susan pulled back, looked to her side, and reached for a piece of paper towel that sat folded on the table. She spread it flat. Then she drew a long horizontal line with a pen and pushed the paper toward her father.

"Bisect the line."

"What?"

"Just make a mark. Midpoint."

"This is more Feingold bullshit."

"We're talking about your being an architect. If you're an architect, then you can bisect a line."

"You owe me, Sue. I'm not asking to draw up plans, I just want to get to the site."

"Bisect the line."

Martin took the pen from his daughter and with a clean economy of movement that surprised Brendan, he drew a vertical line through the horizontal. Brendan peered over his brother's shoulder as Martin pushed the piece of paper towel back to Susan.

"And you think that's normal?"

"I think it's fine. I'm fine."

"Jesus, Dad. You just don't see it."

"You don't know the way I can see things now."

"You can't practice like this."

"I have an awareness of space that I didn't have before." He paused. "I don't expect you to understand that."

"What does that mean?"

"You're with them. You wanted me off this project."

"That's . . . that's just so nuts," Susan said, and looked at Brendan for something more than the silence and averted glance that she received.

"It makes sense to me. Jean-Sebastien and Catherine coming to the Dunes. Scouting me. Then you had my license taken away. Better than any noncompete clause."

"The Ordre made a decision. The firm informed them, yes, but Dad, it was necessary for liability reasons. Jean-Sebastien and Catherine didn't do this lightly."

"Yes, yes. They discussed it with you, I know. Painful deliberations. I'm sure it was all very adult and reasoned, but it was still theft."

Susan was silent. She looked at the paper towel. Its ends began to curl up and slowly close over the line she had drawn.

"What do you want, Dad?"

"I want what I'm owed. I want you to recognize that I'm owed something."

"You left the project, Dad," Susan said, and reached out to touch the sleeve of his sweater. "There was an impasse. You and Jean-Sebastien and Catherine decided to part ways. You wanted out. No one forced you out."

Martin shook his head slowly, as though shooing away the thought. "I would have made this project work. With them or by myself."

This was met by silence, with Martin pushing himself away from the table and shifting back and forth in his seat before lifting himself to his feet, trying as much as possible to make the movement look effortless in front of his daughter. Failing.

"I need some air," Martin said to Brendan, "Let me have a moment." Martin maneuvered to the doorway of the room, waved off Brendan's offer to help, and disappeared around the corner and into a hallway.

Brendan realized he should have followed his brother out of the office, but he did not leave. He stayed in the room and felt Susan's glare settle on him. *He should still be at the Dunes.* Susan said nothing, but the message was clear. She seemed a degree sterner now that her father had turned the corner. *You shouldn't let him out like this.* He wanted to say something that excused himself and maybe even something that would remind her that he'd been the one at the bedside, but he was mute in front of her, looking at the bottom row of her front teeth, a wall of perfect tiny incisors, and he imagined her as a four-year-old with milk teeth and then imagined his mother. Still enthralled by her, by the idea of a female Fallon, he was incapable of any reasonable response. He realized, standing in front of his niece, that he would have been hopelessly at the mercy of daughters, a feckless purchaser and boarder of ponies, a down-on-your knees Barbie-man, his best hope of reclaiming any residual Y-chromosome function being the opportunity to play the potentially wrathful nemesis to a host of teenage suitors. He was about to agree with her—the visit had been a disaster and Martin, for all the sympathy lent him by the accident and the moral authority his status as the founding partner had conferred, came off as pretty much a bullying ass. So muteness seemed the best response in the face of her accusations. And even though her exasperation was captivating, he finally felt the need to defend himself. He sat down across the table from her.

"You shouldn't have brought him here," Susan said.

"He's hurt and he's paranoid. If I'd refused to bring him down here, he would've assumed I was just another part of the conspiracy against him." Brendan lowered his voice slightly, perhaps, he thought to himself, in an attempt to sound more believable. "And I thought he had the right to ask you why you had his license suspended."

Susan shook her head. "He's got absolutely no insight, Uncle Brendan." *Uncle Brendan.* Nice. He would have liked a do-over as the uncle.

"He cares about this consulate project, even if it's over for him. The idea for him to be a consultant seemed like an interesting compromise."

"He's half-blind and he's paranoid. He can barely walk. You want someone that impaired involved with your house? With your country's consulate?"

"He only wants to see—"

"He *can't* see."

"You know what I mean. Eventually, he wants to go to the site. Wouldn't that be good PR for the firm?"

"The clients would object."

"The Russians?"

"The Russians. They didn't agree with my father's vision for the project."

"Wasn't his design chosen by the Russians in the first place?"

"Initially, yes, it won the design competition. Then there was a change in the Foreign Ministry; new consular officials arrived with different tastes. The people who were to sign off on the consulate thought the design didn't represent the image that they wanted to project, and they demanded changes."

"Big changes?"

"Starting over. Yeah, the initial design was clearly too eclectic for them. It was like an homage to that Soviet architect he's into: Melnikov. Dad called it a 'modern take on Constructivism,' but the Russians, the new Russians, were totally unimpressed. There was a meeting around Christmas and they came out and said it looked like a spaceship and they wanted something more conventional."

"And he refused."

"He refused."

"And that led to the buyout?"

"Catherine and Jean-Sebastien agreed to modify the project, and they even kept some design elements in it, you know, as a gesture of goodwill to Dad. The last thing they wanted was for him to leave the partnership. But he wasn't prepared to change one thing, a real line-in-the-sand ultimatum, and he let the Russians and Catherine and Jean-Sebastien know. The firm was going to lose the project." Brendan nodded and wondered where Martin was at that moment, staggering into some fresh provocation or maybe just standing outside his old office, the loss settling in and becoming more than just a contractual detail. Becoming real. Susan folded the paper towel that Martin had drawn on. "He's at home now?"

"We got back yesterday."

"How's he doing?"

"He likes to have the lights out. A couple of times at the Dunes, I found him on all fours, crawling around his room. I thought he'd fallen, but he was down there, sort of exploring."

"Oh God. Does he have appointments to go to or something?"

"In a couple of weeks. An assessment at a rehab center here in town and some medical appointments. He's supposed to meet with a psychiatrist, as well."

"I think that would be a really good idea."

"His psychologist from the rehab center told me it's pretty standard following a head injury to have depression," Brendan said, and then continued. "Before the accident, he was okay?"

"Sure. If anything, he was defiant. He spilt with Agnetha over a year ago, but he seemed genuinely relieved after that ended. Things around here were stressful, even before the buyout, but you have to know my dad; he doesn't shy away from things like that."

"He didn't talk about anything?"

"Not really," Susan replied, interrupted by a noise outside in the hallway, causing both of them to look toward the doorway that Martin had recently passed through. "That's just him, though. Or maybe it's a Fallon thing. Maybe you could tell *me.*" She squeezed his arm. "Thank you for coming to stay with him. With Mom away, it would have been impossible for me to look after all this. And Norah, well, she—"

Brendan, magnanimous, waved her off: "You're welcome."

"No one expected you to do this."

He tried not to sound offended. "All the more reason, then."

Susan looked at him for a moment, a facial gesture that made him think of his sons in Portland. They had never known their cousins. For a moment, he thought about all the things that were unknown in his life, and how the discovery of those things never considered led to what felt like a pang of loss.

"You should get him out of here. I don't think it's going to be good for him."

Brendan nodded at this.

After a short and frantic search, Brendan found Martin stalled in a corridor outside the lunchroom. Martin was standing silently at the end of the hallway, facing a window that, when Brendan looked over his brother's shoulder, he could see overlooked an intersection. A blue-and-white city bus briefly rolled to a stop in the gap between buildings, and its appearance cheered Brendan, as he thought that Martin was watching, capable of taking it in. But then Brendan looked down and saw his brother's feet shuffling under him, the effort without advance, someone in the water, struggling just to stay afloat.

Chapter 8

Martin's hands wandered over surfaces, mapping out the dimensions of new territory. *Paris,* he said to himself, and his right hand lingered on one of the corners of the model that sat before him on the table. The northwest corner, he thought—he could see it so clearly (*see* was the wrong word, but then again, it was the only word, a word defiled for so long by the eyes when it meant knowledge and experience).

The comforting certainties of the model, lifted onto the kitchen table by Brendan, were a respite after a rancorous day, which had ended with the futility of a dozen cold calls to lawyers in search of some way to invalidate the buyout deal, reinstate him with the Ordre, and take back control of the firm. The law firm that F/S+H retained refused even to take his call, which told him that Jean-Sebastien and Catherine had been there already. With the legal avenues seemingly exhausted, Martin deployed plan B and tried to contact Tony Cheng, the senior project manager for the consulate, only to hit an unexpected wall of voice mail. Tony was not a voice-mail guy, Martin said glumly, explaining to Brendan that he had once called his associate for a relatively unimportant question, only to reach him at his mother's funeral. No answer on Susan's phone, and the receptionist at St. Joseph/Houde was not picking up, either. Total call screening. He felt quarantined.

The model helped to calm him down. But it was more than a

distraction. The model was space he could understand, an intersection of shape and memory, a revelation in the dark. Martin turned, hearing his brother near, feeling Brendan's gaze on him, on the model.

"I built it."

"Very nice. One of your designs?"

Martin gave his head a shake. "Oh, no. Someone else's. But I built the model."

"It's nice anyway. Precision work." He could feel Brendan move closer, at his right shoulder now. "What is it?"

"A building designed for an exhibition in the 1920s. Torn down a few months after it was built."

"Modern, right?"

Martin was reminded of every science-fair project he'd ever completed; the cursory visit of the school principal, who gave the impression he knew your disciplinary record more clearly than your name.

"Modern? Sort of. Like saying a Chihuahua's a dog."

Brendan was unfazed. "Do you remember building that?"

Martin nodded, surprised at his answer as the words left his lips. "I suppose I built it in the last year. It stuck with me."

The index finger of Martin's right hand moved up the stairs of the pavilion. With the pad of his finger, he navigated to the very point where Melnikov would have stood for his famous photo. Martin took his hands away from the model and opened his eyes, and the clarity of the steps and the facade itself were obliterated, bleached in a light so intense it could have been straight from a Los Alamos daybreak. Melnikov was gone, too, his work dismantled again.

"Funny what sticks with a person," Brendan said, turning away.

It took three trips down to the garage to pack the car the

following morning, and with each elevator ride, Martin had made it a point to accompany his brother, as if suspicious that Brendan was secretly dumping his belongings instead of loading the trunk of the Lexus. All this was the eventual result of Martin's announcement that he wanted to get out of the city, away from the firm and any thoughts of the consulate. Martin tried to rationalize it as the necessary change of scenery (after only a couple of nights at home, on the heels of several months in a rehab hospital, this struck Brendan as patently false, but he understood the therapeutic value of distance after witnessing the humiliations, some admittedly self-inflicted, that his brother had gone through).

This decision was also a relief for Brendan. He'd been forced to listen to an unremitting stream of his brother's lonely-drunk defiance as he left F/S+H, followed by a sustained invective about his colleagues—Susan not escaping the harsh judgment—that segued into monologue about the lack of loyalty and the complete absence of gratitude. After all this, the suggestion to leave town seemed like the sanest decision that his brother could make. No distractions, no registered letters or obsessed-about former workplaces with their own threats of restraining orders. Besides, after less than forty-eight hours in Montreal—a city he was coming to associate with Martin's squabbles and disappointments and the nuts and bolts of providing some form of custodial care—Brendan himself was already fingering the car keys.

The car was packed (stuffed to the gills with boxes of notes that Martin made him bring, along with the architectural model, which needed to be fitted into the trunk with more delicacy than any animal birth demanded) and it was only once they were on the road that Brendan had a cascade of second thoughts. What if Martin became ill out there in the bush? A seizure maybe, or just if he wandered off. Was the cabin opened up, or even habitable?

(Was there even a cabin? Martin had given him the key and a theoretical address, but that was just *a* key, and for all he knew it could have been the key to a locker at a downtown health club.) Lastly, he had trusted Martin to know the address and a rough idea of directions, and only now, on the road, was he beginning to wonder about their veracity, coming from a brain that had gone through its share of commotion. Susan was right. He couldn't say no. Brendan hoped this wasn't due to pity, and he tried to reconfigure the rationale into one where he was capable of recognizing his brother's grievances, where he shared some of the sense of loss and exclusion and even abandonment. And finally, the trump card: They were family, and what did those bonds mean if not to allow the occasional exercise of questionable judgment in support of a deeper, less explicable sentiment?

Without any help from Martin, Brendan finally found his way to the Champlain Bridge and continued on Highway 10 straight east. Traffic at midmorning was surprisingly heavy, and then it thinned out, and from that point he felt a relief that the open road provides to those who ruminate too long and hard. He sensed that Martin felt the same way (although there was no way of proving it; his brother was silent and affectless in the passenger seat). But traveling east with Martin beside him, he began to feel as though he was doing the right thing.

"Hatley?" Brendan said speculatively. He looked at the GPS monitor, which only told him he was headed east and the destination was left "unknown." "Not getting any results for Hatley."

"Try 'North Hatley.'"

"Okay, anything in the Hatley metropolitan area," Brendan said as he reentered the destination onto the screen. It blinked back a map and an ETA. "Thanks," Brendan said. There was no response from Martin, sunglasses on again, the fingers of his right hand maneuvering up and down the line of buttons of his shirt, the laborious attempts at a clarinet solo only he could hear.

Even when Brendan was a teenager, he was forever hearing from his mother that Martin needed looking after. "Susceptible," she would say in that way that made you realize she had a ready-for-broadcast two-hour supporting lecture if you chose to disagree with her diagnosis. It was his mother's contention that Martin was easily swayed, and she shook her head when she said this, as though dismayed that genetics or environment had conspired against her second son to weaken the Scots backbone that had managed to see their people through difficult times. Brendan always appreciated that she never ventured it was the diluted Irish blood they got from their father.

Whatever the case, his mother confided to him that summer he was called up for service that she was worried about Martin. It was the sixties and Martin was seventeen and Brendan thought his mother's concerns were probably no different from those of the mother of any teenager anywhere else in America at that time. His mother even advanced the notion of drugs (she'd been reading about it, she told him, her eyebrow arching as he imagined the *Ladies' Home Journal* exposé that had planted the thought).

He reassured her, of course. Not out of a deeper understanding of his brother, nor simply because reassuring her seemed the most important thing to do, but because the evidence indicated otherwise. A good kid, good in school, talking about college in the long term, not mentioning Vietnam but signing up for ROTC, just like his older brother; all of it made Brendan assume that Martin was just like him, that they shared beliefs and he would do the right thing. He reassured his mother again that Martin was fine, and maybe she took his words to heart too completely. To her credit, she put none of it back in his face when she wrote him to tell him what Martin had done. By that time, Brendan was twelve time zones away and the news that Martin was leaving for Canada hit like mortar fire. His mother's letter was made up of details, telegraphic, as though her disbelief didn't allow for adjectives, much less emotion. She wrote that Martin had left without warning in August, crossing over the border to Canada. He'd written her from Montreal, where he had found a place and was registering for school and applying for refugee status. There was no other explanation, except to say that he wasn't coming back.

Nowhere in his mother's letter was there a mention of her, or their father's, disappointment at receiving the news. No anger. Not a word about losing a son, just as there was no consideration of the legal consequences of draft evasion or possible imprisonment should he come home. Just details, like a travel itinerary.

The little bastard. The little fucking bastard. Remembering his reaction to the letter was still capable of provoking something in Brendan now, nearly forty years later. Something more than rage. The visceral response to betrayal. The physical feeling of being clubbed by someone's repudiation. *Your values mean nothing; your example means nothing.* The sun beating down as the pages of the letter crimped in his hands and the deep, air-gnashing ambient howl of C-130s. *You are a fool.*

He got rid of the letter immediately, but of course it stayed with him. In a way, it made the next weeks and months easier, providing him with a little wellspring of rage to call on to get through the more trying times. He knew what guys in his company felt like when they got a letter from their girlfriends, dumping them. The best way he could describe the feeling would be to say it gave him an appetite for fighting, and in lieu of gunfire, it turned something otherwise as absurdly geopolitical as a foreign war into the more understandable feeling of a personal grudge.

The anger made it easier to eat shit, to tolerate the boredom and the arterial bursts of terror, easier to think about shooting. But it also made things more difficult in that it was now clear that if he didn't go home, his parents would have no one returning. In the end, he stopped talking about his kid brother, and nobody much noticed. Everyone had his own war going on.

He looked over to Martin, whose hands moved slowly and systematically, covering over surfaces like a pool vacuum (he had to pay special attention to the hand brake, warding off Martin's wandering left hand on a couple of occasions). Martin was taller than Brendan had remembered him, now more apparent because his brother was upright for increasingly extended periods of time, his stature exaggerated by the sense of risk that accompanied it, that it was a height his unsteady gait could drop him from at any time. The constant reminder that you could pay a price for the simple wish of standing up straight.

"You okay?" asked Brendan.

"Sure. A little tired."

"I wanted to ask you something."

"Go ahead."

"Why did you leave?"

"I didn't think I was going to get any better there."

"No. I'm not talking about the Dunes."

A silence, during which time Brendan thought that his brother might turn around to face him. But he remained pressed up against the passenger-side door, as if something had been lost in the side-view mirror.

"Oh. Do we have to talk about this now?"

"I thought it was as good a time as any."

"Thousands of people didn't go to Vietnam. I thought it was obvious. I didn't believe in the war."

"I suppose I never understood. . . ."

"I think I need to rest."

"Yeah, sure. It's just that when I left Detroit, it seemed like everything was normal. You felt one way and then you changed. I'm curious about when that happened."

"Everything was normal? It was the sixties. Nothing was *normal.* Do you remember the sixties? It was in the news: marches, sit-ins, upheaval. You *do* remember the riots, don't you?"

"I'm not talking about everybody. Or society. I'm talking about you."

"Well, that's your problem right there. The two things aren't separate."

"I just want to know why."

"You don't talk to me *about anything* for nearly forty years, and now you're interested?"

"I need to know."

"Jesus, is this all about *closure*?"

"Stop it."

"Are you seeing a Feingold?"

"Forget it, okay?"

"No, really, are you in therapy? Is this some kind of therapy? I miss America sometimes, you know. You're a totally sensitive people now. All therapied up."

"I don't know why I even brought this up."

"Because you're still pissed off at me. Because you want to call me a coward or make me feel guilty about how I hurt Mom and Dad. But you don't want to make accusations, so you'll bring it up in the hopes that I'll admit to cowardice or betrayal. You can't hit me, so you want 'to talk.' Sensitive people are like that. You should have sent a bunch of counselors to Iraq; you would have had those Sunni motherfuckers waving white flags by the end of the first week."

Martin listened to the words leaving his mouth, the darker pleasures of argument rent by a pang of conscience as he wondered for a moment whether any of Brendan's sons were dodging improvised explosive devices in some Mesopotamian desert. But Brendan is wealthy, he thought. Save for random catastrophe or the tug of easily obtained vice, a rich man's children are usually safe inside America, tucked deep inside layers of America. Whatever sympathy Martin had for his brother dissolved as he sensed Brendan formulating the next question.

"Because whatever happened to you, it never happened to me. I suppose I wanted to know if it was me. Was it just because I went first?"

"I don't understand what you're talking about."

"Did you see something in me that scared you or made you think it was a mistake to go?"

"No."

"Was I scared?"

"You're asking me?"

"Yeah. Did I seem scared to you? "

Martin shook his head and looked away. He said "No" plainly to the passenger's side window. Past the window he thought he could see gray sky taking up more of the horizon than it should and he took off his glasses as the sky began to shift. The sky then fell away completely, its cloud cover now reduced to smudges and smears, the sky nothing more than the aluminum sidewall of a tractor-trailer that was making the same journey at roughly the same speed.

Chapter 9

Martin reached for the one of the precision controls on the car's door and tickled it into giving him a little more air through the window. A thin jet of warmth, even at this hour in the morning. Late July outside, flooding into the car, building with an energy he could appreciate even as they cleaved through it like a speedboat.

He thought about Feingold's advice back at the Dunes, how unnecessary it was for her to ask him to concentrate on the linear; hell, the linear wouldn't leave him alone. But he imagined it would be a linear stretching forward, something created by him. He would have his office at F/S+H back and have another chance to get out to the consulate site. He had allowed himself the fantasy of Susan as his surrogate, an extension of him, someone he could trust to tell him how things were progressing.

But instead, the linear streamed off like contrails behind him: things said a minute before, some sensory experience, a memory of all the things he was trying to convey about Melnikov, the sound of Brendan's voice, the threads of linear arranging themselves into some odd fabric of a life that had some semblance to his. All it took was one innocent statement to start him off now, get him rolling down some hill into a pasture of mysteriously retrieved memories. He was neither happy nor sad that Brendan had dredged up the past, but simply amazed at the ease with which memories emerged from what was said. He could not stop the linear now.

A summer day in Montreal, crowds swarming around him, separating him from his family. Martin stood almost exactly between the United States and the Soviet Union. If he faced one way, he could see Buckminster Fuller's huge geodesic dome that acclaimed America. The other direction offered the swooping roof of the Soviet pavilion. He had a memory of being able to appreciate both pavilions at the same time if he positioned himself between them on the footbridge that connected Ile Sainte-Hélène and Ile Notre-Dame. But that seemed impossible now, he thought to himself, that memory must have been a construction itself.

His mother and father were off somewhere at another pavilion, probably eating something exotic whose name neither could pronounce. They had all agreed to meet on this particular bridge at 2:30 if they were separated. Brendan had been beside him just a moment before, but they had lost sight of each other, and now Martin stood alone, feeling like a stone in a stream of people. The sun shone: How was it that he could not recall the brightness of the day, but only the heat on his skin? Why was it that memory was registered in such a way? Always heat more than light. He stood there on the bridge, afraid to be alone and at the same time exhilarated by the movement of the crowd around him.

They had driven up to Montreal from Detroit two days before, checked into the motel that night, and arrived at the Expo gates at dawn to meet the throngs with identical plans. He had spent weeks reading about Expo, the islands that had been dredged into existence to form the site in the middle of the St. Lawrence River, the monorails and pavilions and endless streams of visitors. The experience disoriented him; it was one of the few times in his life that reality dwarfed expectations. He could not have envisaged the scale or the pace or the beauty, and he spent that first day dumbfounded, getting lost and found, staring at buildings whose shapes were impossible and inevitable at the same time. He spent an hour on the banks of the nearby Cité de Havre, studying the heaping cubed miracle of l'Habitat, built by some architecture student a little more than ten years older than he. He lined up to pass through the pavilions that seemed to alternate between defying gravity or convention or both and the limits of imagination. He walked across islands where none had existed five years earlier. This was all normal; this was progress. This was the future. His future.

Brendan then appeared beside him, facing away, oblivious to how close they were, mesmerized by the crowd, as well. His neck was recognizable to Martin; formerly pale from the recent shave he'd gotten, a neck now reddening in the sunlight of the day. A neck thickly muscled. A man ready for battle. His brother, he remembered hearing his father say, had a military bearing. In two weeks, Brendan would test that notion, shipping out to Camp Pendleton before flying across the Pacific. The trip to Expo had been Brendan's concession to their parents, a last family gathering. It had taken some fast talking at the border crossing at Sarnia to get Brendan across the border, the thought of a soon-to-be infantryman slipping into Canada just before deployment to Vietnam was bound to rouse some suspicion, but who dodges the draft with their parents and little brother in tow? Besides, the border guards understood. Maybe Brendan had always been able to charm border guards. Everyone wanted to go to Expo that summer. They were waved through. Have a good trip and Godspeed, they said.

Brendan turned, registering no surprise that he should find Martin there among the other 100,000 people. "Where're the folks?" he asked, and Martin just shrugged. Brendan looked relaxed, both hands on the railing of the bridge.

Finish high school and go to war. It would have seemed

arbitrary and harsh to someone else, but to the Fallons, this was simply how the future was constructed, a plan survived and endorsed by their father. And now Jim Fallon's boys would serve their country, too. That was the unspoken expectation, and so it was Reserve Officers' Training Corps for both of them and a call-up now for Brendan. This was more than normal, Martin tried to reassure himself; this had been *necessary.* This was how his parents had met; this was, indirectly, how he'd come into being. This was the generational experience of Fallons in America, the return from a foreign war to start an adult life. His grandfather had served in the First World War, surviving combat, only to succumb to the Spanish influenza epidemic that swept through the Corktown tenements of Detroit the year after he returned. (In the annals of their family history, his grandfather's death was nonetheless consecrated as a "military death" for its temporal proximity to the war, along with its absurd fulfillments; the suddenness and randomness, the tragedy of a young family—including Martin's father, then aged three—left behind.) There was also the vaguer history of a great-uncle enlisting and dying in the Spanish-American War, another story conscripted to reinforce the feeling of some familial destiny, which, to Martin, came to seem more and more like a genetic disorder, expressed as a penchant for uniforms and marching, a resignation to travel for business purposes and a shortened life expectancy.

With the river below and all the tourists around them, Martin had been able to forget the thought of his brother's imminent departure, but having Brendan appear beside him was a reminder, his presence paradoxically making his absence more real. *Don't go*, Martin wanted to say, but he wasn't sure if it was for Brendan or for him, the next Fallon in line for a haircut and a chopper ride deep into some jungle. And so they stood on the bridge and looked at the river and said nothing. Martin looked at his watch. It was 2:30 P.M. on July 22, 1967. Their parents would arrive soon.

They were all likely still asleep in their motel when it started back in Detroit. According to the story—the *story,* and what was that except the most resilient of all the threads of gossip that emerged?—a police car was dispatched to break up an after-hours party on Twelfth Street, expecting to round up the typical four or five diehards. When they opened the door to the club, one of the officers immediately called for backup, realizing that there must have been more than fifty people inside. Squad cars and paddy wagons arrived and everyone inside the booze can was arrested, causing onlookers in the predominantly black neighborhood to congregate and express their opposition. The police report made reference to a party, an illegal gathering where liquor was being consumed without the proper permit. What no one said at the outset was the reason for the party. This was a lesser thread of the story. Months later, it would come out that it was a welcome-home gathering held for two vets returning from Vietnam.

Years later, Martin would understand that the cumulative forces of an altercation, the determinants of escalation or resolution, are difficult to gauge immediately. The push and pull of bodies, sheer crowd numbers, the anger of a crowd fed by something as noble as a sense of an injustice unanswered or as banal as too much alcohol and boredom. Police understand all this explicitly; the call for backup is one of the most natural reactions to an acknowledged threat. So are the displays and deployment of the symbols of physical authority. A phalanx of riot shields. Nightsticks, firearms, horses, if you have them. Control the dynamics of the crowd; control the situation. A balance of forces: order versus chaos from one side, repression versus freedom as seen from the other. Something happened on Twelfth Street in Detroit on the morning of the twenty-third that did not allow for the crowd to disperse and that prevented everyone from just going home to their beds. By morning, Detroit was in flames.

The Fallon family spent that next day, Sunday, July 23, enjoying Expo, oblivious. Governor Romney and Mayor Cavanaugh embargoed the news of their burning city as long as they could (while at the same time appealing to President Johnson to declare a state of emergency and send in federal troops to restore order), and so it wasn't until Monday, the twenty-fourth, that news of what was going on in Detroit was organized into a story that could be put on the front page of every evening newspaper in the United States. It was Brendan who discovered what was going on, inadvertently, by picking up a copy of the *Montreal Star* and trying to find out if the Tigers had beaten the Orioles the night before, only to find that the game had been postponed "due to civil emergency." On the front page, under a story describing the arrival that day of President Charles de Gaulle in Montreal, was a description of the chaos that had engulfed Detroit, accompanied by an aerial photo of the city, showing dense columns of smoke tilting to the northeast.

That night, with copies of the *Star* and the *Montreal Gazette* clamped under his arm, Jim Fallon spent hours on the pay phone in the motel's parking lot, trying to get hold of anyone who would answer in Detroit to tell him the fate of his electrical-supply store on Highland Avenue. Martin waited beside him, swatting away shadflies under the streetlight as Brendan and his mother packed for their premature trip home. His father phoned the store, and Martin assumed there was no answer, but the look on his father's face told him that there hadn't even been the consolation of hearing the phone ring. Brendan came out of the motel to tell them that the television news was reporting that the state police had been called in, and Martin remembered how they'd all stood around, straining to view this as good news.

They drove the nine hours back to Detroit in a paralytic silence, and it was only years later that Martin found out from his mother that his father had finally gotten through to one of his employees and found out the fate of the store that night—it had been razed, along with twenty square blocks of the Highland Avenue neighborhood where it used to stand. The sky above the Detroit River was the color of charred salmon the morning they arrived, and they were rerouted through an endless maze of barricades, until they arrived at their house in Farmington Hills around noon the next day. Martin's father disappeared for the rest of the day, taking Brendan with him on his sortie into the city, returning late that evening but refusing to talk, refusing to watch television or answer the phone, which kept ringing. His mother wouldn't speak, either, as if to honor the pledge her husband had made. The house was silent but buzzed with the unfocused but organizing energy of an electrical storm about to break.

It was Brendan who told him what he had seen down on Highland Avenue, that even with a National Guard escort, they'd only been able to get within a few blocks of the store site. But what they'd seen had been enough. The block was gone, carbonized, as if it had been downtown Dresden. Looters had ravaged anything that had survived along the periphery. Martin remembered watching Brendan describe what he had seen. It was for the best, Brendan reasoned in that way that riots and darkness seemed to be demanding of people, that the store was already gone. Otherwise, their father would certainly have held vigil in what remained of their store, the sniper fire and specter of looters little more than a nostalgic whiff of his time in the Ninth Army—that is, until they came to the door with their guns, their plans. Yes, in that way, maybe they were lucky. Now, there was no evidence that Fallon's Electrical had ever existed, Brendan said, and as he said this, Martin paid closer attention, studying his brother, as he could have sworn he saw a trace of satisfaction in the expression he wore, trying to discern if this was some sort of preparatory response to a personal wound, part of a soldier's training.

And then, three days later, with his hometown still smoldering and half the population in open revolt, Brendan shipped out for Camp Pendleton. His father wouldn't hear of his son's trying to defer the inevitable.

Over the next few days, a parade of insurance adjusters visited the house, commercial mourners who sat at the kitchen table with their open briefcases and spoke with his father about settlements and time lines. Cutting a check could only soften the blow so much. Jim Fallon's store was gone; stock was gone. But it was more than that. He had fifteen employees without a place to work or a paycheck for the foreseeable future. Federal troops had arrived—a persistent rumor among the white merchants who lost everything was that Johnson had delayed deployment in an effort to cripple any presidential ambitions Governor Romney might have as they headed into an election year—replacing the weekend soldiers who made up the National Guard. Snipers were flushed out and the city was gradually reclaimed.

On the radio and television, news reporting ceased and opinions began. The popular verdict at first was that this was simply a criminal insurrection, with any mention of race or poverty absent from the discussion. But almost immediately, new details emerged and alternative analyses arose, none of them as simple or as reassuring to Martin as the thought that this was nothing more than the act of bad men committed against innocent shopkeepers and the forces of order.

Now Martin was faced with the assertion that the riot was a reaction to excessive police force or that it was the response to poverty. More personal to the Fallons, who had made the move north of Eight Mile Road ten years before, was the allegation that the riot was the inevitable result of the white middle class's abandonment of downtown Detroit. Martin had understood their move only in the personal terms of how his parents had explained it: a bigger house for two growing boys, a garden for their mother. Nothing more complicated than the modest success of middle-class America.

Martin understood, perhaps only fully years later, when the decline of Detroit was an accepted fact, the textbook study of decay and urban blight, that his father viewed the destruction of the Highland neighborhood in general and of Fallon Electrical in particular not just as an act of violence perpetrated against him but also as an act of betrayal. A repayment for the hubris that a person could ignore or perhaps even withstand the reality of demographic change. When Martin had remembered the store on Highland Avenue, he liked to imagine that it was an island of decency, black and white people working together, and that his father treated all who came through the door with all the sincerity and goodwill that a Great Society demanded of its citizens. But he lived in Farmington Hills by then, in a room of his own, with a lawn and a bike and no real working knowledge of the lives of those who lived on Twelfth Street or Highland Avenue.

Fallon Electrical reopened two months later in a commercial district of Farmington Hills, the newly hired staff as uniformly white as the customers, and no one ever spoke of Highland Avenue again. There was never any mention of the riots or the workers left behind when the Highland Avenue store was razed. Everyone he knew tried to carry on and make reassurances. The lawns of Farmington Hills continued to be watered and mown and, as usual, school started just after Labor Day.

There must have come a point, Martin thought, when he crossed the line from thinking of his family as blameless victims to understanding that they were not. He wondered if it could be narrowed down to a moment, some impression or word spoken that tipped the scales. But there was nothing. No epiphanies. All he could remember was the silence of his house after Brendan left, the impression that it must have occurred here, in the incubator of that silent house, an awareness dawning.

He tried to imagine an alternate life for himself, one where he would be allowed to continue to think of his father as a hero, or at least a victim of the July riot. It wouldn't have been so difficult; many people felt this way in the aftermath. This would have been possible even if his father had said something, but there was only silence, big Fallon silence—and Martin could never be sure how much was caused by the loss of the business and what was due to Brendan's departure. A more charitable son would have perhaps acknowledged the loss his father felt, would have considered its complicated nature. Maybe, Martin thought, that this was all just a result of confluences, that had his brother not gone off to the war at the same time, or if it had occurred in 1962 and not in 1967, the outcome would have been fundamentally different.

But Brendan was gone and it was 1967 and his parents and Farmington Hills offered nothing but silence, which seemed, to Martin, ridiculous and servile and deeply false. To have gone on living as they did, Martin would have needed his father to admit that something was deeply wrong with the way they lived, that he would have to have had the strength of character to make such an admission. An act of courage more robust that accepting an insurance check and walking away.

Martin doubted that he could have been talked out of whatever changes he underwent that year—perhaps a constant argument would have only solidified the newfound opposition to everything his family stood for—but the silence was license. For a seventeen-year-old, the silence was freedom enough to allow him to conclude that the way he felt was not simply opposition but also consciousness, an awareness. It was a consciousness that recast the events of the summer of 1967, showing his parents as part of a society that hadn't suffered the riot as much as created the conditions that made it inevitable and yet somehow conspired to allow them to claim further victimhood. Detroit, his Detroit, the city he had grown up in and been proud of and believed in, had never really existed. Detroit was an ugly armed camp that he had known nothing about, that he hadn't cared enough to understand. And at this thought, Farmington, his bedroom, the municipal park greenery and barbecues and suburban idyll all seemed at once a huge conceit, as flawed as their old imaginings of a shining city on the river, more flawed for having no aspiration to justice or anything more noble than the fact that it was miles removed from Detroit.

Martin Fallon radicalized in the summer and fall of 1967, as suburban teenagers do, minute by poolside minute, emerging with absolute certainties about the world whose veils had had been torn away. Nothing about him had changed, he would argue, except that he felt *aware,* and that changed everything. The riot was a revolution to him, and no amount of green space or reassurance or insurance money or zombie smiles from his parents could hide the fact that he was now aware of poverty and race. He was aware of force, how it was used, and on whose behalf.

In the autumn of 1967 he came to understand his country as an imperial power, a devouring beast that fed off the constant sacrifice of its hypnotized citizens, in which people like his parents not only condoned, but demanded that their elder son take innocent life and risk his own in a useless foreign war. And they would demand that Martin go next. For Martin to go to war would be to accept this as right, as moral, as somehow truthful.

He decided he would not go.

He told no one. Once the decision was made, the next step meant that Martin would have to leave—he would be forced to register for the draft when his eighteenth birthday came around in August—and when he considered the options, the answer sat conveniently on his desk, a souvenir from his summer vacation, calling out to him in the form of a pamphlet that featured a monorail and a huge metallic sphere and the promise of sanctuary. Sunlight and his brother beside him, studying the brown legs of girls in summer dresses. The necessary other place. Conveniently, another country. He picked up the pamphlet. Even now, he could remember the colors and the shape of the Expo logo, Montreal's silhouette behind, embracing it. He remembered the slogan, the call to leave everything that he had come to revile, to embrace something larger, to start again: *Come visit the world!*

Chapter 10

Three-quarters of the way through the drive, as the intensity of his brother's fidgeting began to coincide with the swells of his own impatience, Brendan decided to pull the car off the highway, easing onto the long exit ramp that fed one of the roadside restaurant/gas station clusters that divided the journey into intervals.

Brendan installed Martin at an outside picnic table and went inside for something to drink, pivoting to check on him from a line whose snaking length seemed more fitting for Stones tickets or some vital commodity made scarce by an inept five-year plan than for two cups of coffee.

When he returned, Martin was gone.

Brendan scanned the outdoor eating area around the restaurant, deserted save for an employee emptying a garbage can and a young couple ring-mastering their toddlers into position for a meal. The parking lot was an orderly riot of cars and tractor-trailers. No sign of Martin.

Brendan doubted his brother would have been able to negotiate that pedestrian no-man's-land without the trumpet of a car horn to greet him. He reasoned Martin must have gone into the restaurant while he'd been occupied at the register, to look for him, to use the toilet maybe, but a search inside—a lap through the dining room, followed by a quick inventory of footwear visible under the stall doors of the washroom—yielded nothing.

How fast could Martin walk? He'd lost visual contact for no more than a few minutes, and even in a straight line Martin didn't seem capable of mustering the necessary land speed for escape. (This is what he'd been reduced to, he thought, calculating search perimeters like some hapless southern warden, lacking only the yodeling scent-hounds and a photo of the fugitive.)

It was when he came back out of the restaurant complex, a cup of coffee still in each hand, that Brendan spotted his brother a hundred yards away, visible in the small gully of space between two tractor-trailers, limping toward a busy highway.

He put the coffees down and ran, slaloming through the parked cars, all the while trying to keep an eye on Martin, cutting down the distance, when suddenly his brother, out in the open a moment before, disappeared from view.

He shouted Martin's name and imagined the family at the picnic table turning around, the kids alert to the novelty of a voice raised at someone else, the parents nostalgic for the containable dramas of a purely adult world. At the edge of the parking lot, Brendan came upon a large grassy ditch that separated the highway from the restaurant complex. Martin stood at the very bottom of the ditch, slowed by waste-high grass, uncertain terrain, and maybe even his brother's voice.

"Where are we?" Martin asked.

Brendan was breathless. He staggered down the embankment. "What the hell are you doing?"

"I just needed to walk."

"Onto the highway?"

"Where are we?" Martin repeated, a tone of desperation in his voice this time, as if Brendan were playing with him.

"Maybe twenty miles from Hatley," Brendan said.

"This is Highway Fifty-five, right?"

"Yeah. I think we hit the one-oh-eight just up ahead."

"It was around here." Brendan looked around, baffled by his brother. "The accident. You told me it was by the one-oh-eight, that it was around here."

"Must have been someone else who told you that. I only know that you were heading west on the one-oh-eight."

"Okay," Martin said, turning in the ditch reeds. He peeked over the crest of the ditch, as if trying to scout out a predator on the distant savanna. "I was headed west, toward Montreal?"

"Well, not headed west. Pointed west."

"Pointed west?"

"You weren't headed anywhere. You were parked on the shoulder."

Martin turned in Brendan's general direction. "That makes no sense."

"It was a surprise to the guy driving the snowplow, too."

"Was he hurt?" Martin asked in a voice that surprised Brendan with its tone of general alarm. Brendan studied the expression on his brother's face—wide-eyed and unfocused, suggestive of something being played out behind them.

"He was okay; I'm pretty sure of it. Let's get out of this ditch."

They both sidestepped up the embankment, Brendan behind his brother, an arm extended and a hand opened in preparation for a possible fall.

"I was coming from the cabin, then."

"Probably. Who knows . . ."

"Did you speak with the police?"

"I did."

"What did they say?"

"They told me they see it all the time. Some fall asleep; some have had a couple of beers."

"But they're *in* the ditch. I was pulled over on the shoulder. Why was I stopped?"

"Look, Martin, I don't know."

"This was February, right?" Brendan nodded. "I almost never go to the cabin in the winter. Did I have car trouble?"

"The police told me that there were no calls from your cell that night. Maybe you were just tired."

"Bullshit. I was a half hour from the lake house. I wouldn't have stopped. I wouldn't have stopped on the shoulder."

Martin said this as they crested the gully. He stopped and turned, assessing the ditch again, appearing to Brendan as though he were disappointed not to find his car keys in the long grass. "I wouldn't have stopped. Not here." Martin's voice rose, seeming to Brendan to have the same tonal quality, the same visceral timbre, of an animal in distress. It was a sound that touched him, almost more than the fact that it came from his brother. The sound demanded action, or at least an accounting for why that action was not taken. "Someone did this to me."

"Stop it, Martin." Brendan said with enough force that he immediately looked around them and saw that the children of the family at the picnic table were watching the drama, faces frozen, while their parents' heads snapped back to the lunch on the table before them. "The police told me that the snowplow driver came over a crest. He didn't see you. He had no warning."

"No, not *him.* I was going someplace at a time I wouldn't usually be going, I was stopped in a place I would never have stopped. Isn't that suspicious to you?"

Brendan listened to his brother, an arm on his shoulder, wordlessly trying to guide him back, coaxing him away from the unrelenting stream of highway traffic and noise. A career as a veterinarian had convinced him of the transformative power of information, just as it had endowed him with what he believed to be a reliable sense of how and when to dispense it. Some people needed to know the truth about the lump in their dog's neck, and other clients would tell him in innumerable, subtle ways that they couldn't bear to have that discussion. Not yet. And here, on the side of a highway with Martin, stumbling with his brother through a wasteland of memory and loss and Russian architects, Brendan again weighed the options of telling Martin more. On the day he arrived at the trauma center in Montreal, Brendan had met with a police officer who told him that a roll of duct tape and a garden hose had been found in the trunk of Martin's crumpled BMW, both items still in their cellophane and further sealed in their place by the force of the snowplow's impact with the vehicle. The officer, a young woman who dropped down into a seat beside Brendan in the ICU's waiting room, reported all these details in matter-of-fact copspeak, as though rehearsing the sequence of details and precise wording of the unabridged report that could have been written, all without advancing any conclusion of her own. Facts. Just the ellipses of circumstances and duct tape and a man alone in his car on the side of a country road on a February night. The officer then left the waiting room, probably assuming whatever family members she spoke to would either have enough insight to infer their loved one's intention or that they wouldn't care. Brendan fell into neither category, and so the implications of what was found in the car staggered him: On that highway shoulder back in February, his brother had considered ending his life and had either decided against using the duct tape and hose or had been interrupted before he could put them to use. Had he been in the midst of ending his life or refusing to do so? For Brendan, understanding what had actually happened to his brother was reduced to a dilemma—binary, existential and unknowable now that the only person who truly knew had had his intention scraped clean by the blade of a snowplow.

And so, in the weeks and months of recovery that followed, Brendan had observed his brother for any sign of that original intention. The awareness of what he had wanted. *It will come to him,* Brendan thought; *it needs to come from him.* But no memories emerged. No signs appeared. Martin only stumbled and raged, offering no easy answers, half-blind to the world, fully blind to his predicament.

Brendan felt he should say something.

If he said something, it might at least ease Martin's paranoia or calm the ruminations. But it could also make everything worse—trading confusion for the possibility of despair wasn't much of a therapeutic victory—and such a roadside revelation to a brain-injured family member was perhaps not the best plan as they all headed out into the deep woods of wherever they were going.

"Is anything at all coming back from that night?"

"Not really."

They reached the parking lot of tractor-trailers; each vehicle parked a fixed distance from the others. It was quiet, almost contemplative, Brendan thought. A Stonehenge on Highway 55. He looked over, to see his brother studying the asphalt he had to limp across, panting.

"You okay?"

"Someone tried to kill me." He turned to Brendan. "Maybe someone tampered with my car."

"For Christ's sake, listen to yourself talk, Martin. Besides, you didn't make any calls. Which you would have done if you had broken down, right?"

Martin staggered on, not replying, and Brendan could feel a thesis being cobbled together, a web of plots twists from bad television and the rants of sidewalk crazy people. "It was an accident," Brendan said, curtly enough to slap away any other such thoughts.

"I wouldn't have stopped on the side of the road."

"Well, you did."

"It's not like me to do that."

"Look, you did it," Brendan said, instantly aware of his scolding tone. Parental. He adjusted his voice: "Let's say you stopped. No phone calls out. Nothing. You just stop. Why does anybody stop?"

"What do you mean?"

"People stop at the side of the road because they're tired, or maybe they're sick and they need a moment," Brendan said as they passed by the coffee shop and its epic, unresolved line. "Lots of reasons to stop a car. Maybe you were just fed up, Martin."

Martin stopped, his limping gait seeming to seize up in mid-stride. "Fed up? What do you mean?"

"I don't know. Depressed about things."

"Like all this was all my plan, getting hit by a snowplow?"

Brendan raised his hands. "Devil's advocate. You lose your job and give up your partnership, all on the same day that you relinquish control of a project that you had invested yourself in. . . ."

"This wasn't the first project I've lost. That's just business. You can't put your head in an oven just because a job didn't turn out. And you saw the terms of the buyout, Brendan. I came out on top. I rid myself of partners who obviously wouldn't back me up. There wasn't even a noncompete clause in the deal." Brendan studied his brother as he said this, and for the first time he could imagine Martin in charge of something like building a consulate. It was confidence or charisma, like the sun asserting itself against a cloud bank. "I wasn't depressed, Brendan. I was free."

"Okay."

"Do you believe I could do something like that?"

Brendan said *I don't know,* or thought he said it, as he unlocked the car and felt his chest tighten and his shoulders draw up into a gesture that equaled the sentiment. He wanted to be on the road again, to feel the hypnotic calm of velocity and, when he remembered several minutes later and miles away, he was indifferent to the realization that he'd left the coffee behind.

Part II

At last each particle of space is meaningful, Like a syllable of some dismantled word.

—Louis Aragon

Chapter 11

The day's last sunlight escorted them through the streets of North Hatley, sidewalks lightly patrolled by tourists. On the outskirts of town, Brendan had turned on the headlights and stopped by the side of the road, consulting the directions on the screen.

In the silence, Martin sat forward. "There should be a column."

"A column?"

"Yeah. A supporting column. Doric."

"Doric. Good," Brendan said, staring straight ahead. "That helps a lot."

He was lost. Of course, the word had no meaning now that he had a satellite tracking his every move and rolling out bits of the unknown world for him on which to continue. There was no *lost* anymore; there was only following directions or not following directions.

The car bobsledded down the small roads, which were perceptibly narrowing with each curve. It was dark now, the trees around them obscuring twilight, and Brendan strained to make sure he wasn't missing details that could possibly guide them to the cabin. *A column.* Doric, no less. But a column shouldn't be too hard to spot. Maybe there would be a sacrificial altar nearby. And although he was driving down an unnamed road—actually designated *unnamed road* on the GPS, much to Brendan's satisfaction—to an uncertain destination, each gravel road growing narrower, Brendan felt oddly reassured, more certain for the possibilities winnowed down to inevitability. He was as blind as his brother here, as unaware of what lay around the corner, and yet it didn't trouble him like he'd imagined it would.

The column appeared out of the foliage—huge and pale and hovering there starkly in the surroundings. It almost made him laugh. Ten feet tall. Apparently Doric, whatever that meant. Maybe *Doric* meant "bloody huge." The car idled in front of the pillar, Brendan idling with it. How does something like that just appear? Where is it the second before you are aware of it? He then thought for a moment about the sort of person who would drag something like this out into the country, what type of personality had needs that could be addressed only by propping up a couple of tons of marble in the darkness of roadside underbrush. The lower half of the column was wrapped up in some sort of material that appeared to have been torn away in parts.

"Is that metal?"

"Sheet metal," Martin replied as he peered out the window, scanning the ditch just in front of the column.

"Okay," Brendan replied, surprised at how credulous he became once twilight passed.

Brendan pulled the car past the sentinel and into the drive, another road reduced to twinned tire tracks with an intervening median of overgrown grass that tugged at the underside of the car. He drove fifty yards, until the roadway opened into a gravel clearing in front of what looked to be a large farm silo with irregularly placed windows. Brendan stopped the car and eased it into PARK. He stayed in his seat. At this point, Martin leaned forward.

"We're here," Martin said with an offhand assuredness that only irritated his brother.

"I think so," Brendan replied, still peering up at the structure with its lights on. In the darkness, the light was molten, each window a foundry furnace. Another car, a subcompact that glistened in the indeterminate color of reflected light, sat near what looked to be an entry. "Somebody else is here, too."

The key, Martin assured him, was on the ring—one of twenty or so. Finding it would involve the sort of fumbling in the darkness of a doorway that Brendan hoped to avoid. Instead, he stared at the house, trying to see if someone was inside.

"Who's here?" Martin asked as he stepped forward and stumbled on the gravel of the drive.

"I don't know," Brendan replied, and knocked on the door. A couple of neighborly taps and then a good bailiff-quality salvo. Nothing. Brendan stepped back from the door.

"Can you see anybody?"

"Not from here. Can we walk around to the other side?"

"You can't find the key?"

"Someone's in your house, Martin, I just want to see who's here."

"I'm coming, too."

The front facade of the cottage was a two-story wall of galvanized sheet metal. Corrugated, like a Quonset hut tipped on its end. It didn't look rustic. It didn't look like anything Brendan had ever seen. On the way down, Brendan had grabbed glimpses of the other waterfront cabins seen through the trees. *Cabin,* of course, was the wrong word. It didn't take much effort, even looking through the hedges, to see that the lakeside properties weren't cabins or cottages or even chalets, but each one a three-thousand-square-foot, strictly adhered-to homage to a specific lakefront idyll. Brendan was familiar with that style of life, if only from seeing photos of these palaces in design magazines Rita would have sitting around. He'd managed to defuse her exploratory musings about their buying a country house—yes, that was the word, grander, and yet more modest for its Victorian sheen—because all he could see were the pretensions, the unused boathouse and the faux rustic tchotchkes and the board games safely sequestered in some skillfully distressed oxblood cabinet on which the flat-screen TV sat. Besides, since he'd sold the business, they'd begun to travel. They had a great life already. Why would they want to tie themselves down to a McMansion in the woods? Rita probably saw it as a place where the children and the eventual grandchildren would congregate. She must have imagined long weekends and a house full of voices. He hadn't seen fit to grant her even the prospect of that, and so the lights that he saw from those houses were no longer only faint insults to his taste, but had taken on a lingering and more personal admonishment.

"Have you always had this place?" Brendan peered up at the facade, trying to make sense of it.

"Since the late seventies, the land belonged to Sharon's dad. We built on it in the early eighties, when the kids were small."

"You designed it?"

"Of course. Sharon and I take turns with it, alternate summers. But she rarely uses it, so it's pretty much mine."

"Big of her," Brendan said, finding himself smiling. "Most exes would have sold it off or burned it down."

"Well, Sharon's not like that," Martin shot back. "That happen to you?"

"Rita died two years ago."

Martin stopped. He looked over his left shoulder and then straight ahead again. "Mom didn't say anything."

"Mom can't remember much of what either one of us tells her."

"I'm sorry. Why didn't you tell me?"

"You didn't ask."

"I mean at the time."

"I was dealing with it."

"Still."

"What, you'd have come to the funeral?"

"Yeah. Sure."

"You never *met* Rita. You never saw fit to call or to visit. You left me trying to explain who you were to my family and why you weren't part of our lives. You think I'm going to call you for her funeral?" Brendan pulled even with his brother as he said this, the two men standing face-to-face. Up close, Brendan noticed how Martin's eyes darted around, the flailing efforts to see something. Odd animal panic. It almost made him feel ashamed.

"I couldn't go back; you knew that. Why was it up to me to make the first move?" Martin said.

"Because you left . . ."

"I had to leave."

"You didn't just leave; you renounced us."

"I came back for Dad—"

"Day late and a dollar short on that one. . . ."

"—and what did I get for it?"

"I was messed up."

"Yeah, I figured. So drive me back to Montreal if you hate me so much. You're free to go."

"Yeah, I'll just leave you here in the woods."

"Why are you here?"

"What?"

"Why are you here, anyway?"

"We're family."

"Cut the bullshit. It's not like you've been dying to reconnect with *me* over the years."

"I have a respons—"

"Stop it. The truth. Did Mom ask you?"

"I told you, nothing registers with Mom. She still asks about me about Rita and Sharon."

"Is it guilt? Because you can just fuck off about that right now. Fuck off right back to America."

"In case you haven't noticed, you don't have a lot of people clamoring to look after you."

"Thanks."

"I'm sorry," Brendan said. They were both exhausted, Brendan could sense it in their voices. "Here, let me help you."

Martin pushed Brendan's hand away. In the darkness, his brother's movements were surprisingly smooth and his refusal seemed vindicated. He hesitated for a moment, tottering toward what appeared to be a path that led around the structure. Brendan followed, partly out of deference to someone who knew the trail, partly out of a desire to monitor and even catch his brother should his balance fail him.

As dark as the clearing seemed, the path through the trees was deep-space black and silent. Here, on a little path complicated by jutting stones and the exposed roots of surrounding trees, Martin advanced without difficulty, while Brendan stumbled along in his wake. The confines and darkness of the underbrush made him feel suddenly claustrophobic, a thousand hands reaching out from nowhere to brush against them.

The path ended and they came upon the lake, lights along the shoreline doubled into the stitching of a seam of night. Martin kept walking straight ahead down a gentle grade, heading toward the shoreline until Brendan reined him in and turned him around toward the back of the structure.

To their left was a raised patio extending from the back of the building, a promontory from which one could spend hours studying the lake. Whereas the front of the building was clad in sheet metal, the back was walled by glass. It was quite beautiful, more than he'd expected, Brendan realized. A house glowing warm in yellows and greens.

There was a solitary figure on the deck, illuminated and shadowed by the patio lights, facing away from them, not reacting to the commotion of their backwoods stumbling. A head of ponytailed hair, all calipered by headphones. Martin's daughter or the fresh ex-wife maybe. Too young to be Sharon, quite clearly a living saint whose constitution could likely not admit such lounging. Maybe this was the girlfriend, the most recent, just another soon-to-be wreck in his brother's debris field of a personal history. Whoever she was, she sat motionless, dozing or just relaxing to music. They moved closer and Brendan felt dread at the thought of whoever she was being surprised out of the darkness and silence. Brendan stopped as they approached the deck, unwilling to move closer, preferring at that moment to turn around and sit in the car until morning. But at this moment, Martin stuck his head up into the air and moved it ever so slightly, like an adjustment to a satellite dish.

"Norah?" Martin shouted, loudly enough that Brendan winced and they heard the scattering of loons among the echoing of the name along the water. "Norah."

The young woman startled and used both hands to throw off the headphones. She looked over in their direction, to where the voice had come from, obviously unable to fix upon what she was searching for. She stood and walked over to the deck's edge, where she addressed the darkness and whoever happened to be standing in it.

"Dad?" she said, staring into the dark. "Is that you?"

Chapter 12

After Brendan dropped their bags off in the upstairs bedrooms, the three of them gathered in the kitchen, which was easily the most conventional room in the house. An off-season theme park of German-engineered appliances: copper pots and colanders of every conceivable dimension, their sheen attesting to their mostly decorative function, hung in clusters from the ceiling and custom cabinetry that lined the walls. A small kitchen island occupied the middle of the room, with its atoll of stools trailing alongside. Beyond the island, as the kitchen opened up on to the living room, the ceiling simply *ended*. At the edge, a twenty-five-foot ceiling hung over the living room. The kitchen was simply an alcove off this main room, nestled in one of the wings. Beyond windows that made up a wall of the sitting room lay the absolute darkness of Lac Massawippi.

The house was built in the shape of a giant articulated boomerang: a central area, a three-story cylinder, housed the living room and was flanked by two smaller, swooping wings, angled toward the lakefront, creating an enclosed area with a patio. He imagined that from a low-flying aircraft, it must look like the detached prow of an enormous freighter run aground.

Brendan turned down the burner on the stove and coaxed an omelette into existence. Norah, sitting at the island, was watching him handle the pan. He could tell she was hungry. Martin was indifferent, in a corner somewhere, probably touching a wall or sniffing the floor. Brendan was busy trying to concentrate on the omelette.

For Brendan, cooking was the most reliable way of defusing a difficult situation; experiencing the silences between Martin and his daughter after their arrival was enough to make him immediately demand to be shown to the kitchen. At least with Susan, there had been the bond of their work (even if it had been broken and reworked into the source of their argument), but with Norah there seemed to be nothing. After the niceties and twenty seconds of catching up, there was only dead air. But the smell of food filled the spaces and the activity rescued all of them. The perfect form of conflict resolution. It was a wonder that Brendan wasn't a much fatter man.

The fridge had been bare, almost emptier than the one in Martin's abandoned condo. Milk, a few eggs, a lump of cheddar that looked mere minutes away from a color change, and an assortment of fresh vegetables, the only sign of a recent restocking. It would be enough.

Norah was smaller than Susan. Perhaps that was just the impression that came from a person who remained silent. Brendan felt her watch him as he edged and shimmied the pan. With a deft flip, he turned the halves of the omelette against each other. He lifted the omelette and plated it for her. The same color hair, the color he remembered or imagined he remembered on his mother.

"Martin, do you want some?" Brendan asked, and Martin rotated his body to face him. He still had his sunglasses on.

"Is it eggs?"

"Omelette. Western. Universal code word for whatever's in the fridge," Brendan said, and pushed a plate toward Martin. Two hands slid over the counter surface until they encountered the edge of the plate. The right hand followed the edge, moving counterclockwise, the palm of the hand hovering over the omelette. The left hand was motionless, midair. Brendan watched in silence, wondering why the left hand was stalled in space. Eventually, Martin found the utensils and started cutting into the food. Brendan poured what was left of the mix into the pan for his dinner. Norah looked impressed, and Brendan couldn't tell if it was that her father had guessed right about the food and was able to feed himself or if it was the forkful of food she had just lifted to her own mouth.

"Okay?" Brendan asked her.

"Very okay."

"I never really learned to cook." Martin said. "No time."

"Something else for you to learn. It's actually pretty easy," Brendan said at the exact moment things began to go awry. Inattentive to the food in the pan, Brendan had let the omelette, his omelette, cook unevenly, and as he folded it, he already knew that biting into the pockets of semiliquid egg would be his reward for even a moment of culinary hubris. Maybe I'll skip dinner, he thought. He threw together enough vegetables to make a salad and shook the balsamic-looking contents of a bottle over it.

"I didn't think you'd be here," Martin said to Norah.

"I had some work to finish," she replied.

"It couldn't be done in town?"

"It's quiet here. Is it okay that I'm here?"

"Sure. What sort of work?"

"If you want me to go . . ."

"I don't want you to go," Martin said in a low voice, and then raised his head to face Brendan. "She makes films."

"Films? You're making a film here?"

"I make documentaries. I'm editing my latest."

"You can do that here?"

"With the right software and a good-enough laptop, I could do it in a coffeehouse."

"It's nicer here," her father said. "Coffee's free."

Norah watched her father and put her fork down. "Are you okay, Dad?"

Martin paused. "They took away my license. Did you know about it?"

"No."

"Susan didn't tell you?"

"I haven't spoken to her in a few weeks."

"Well, she was in on it. Nice, huh?"

Brendan had salvaged his omelette and put it down on a plate just to the left of his brother. "Martin, she didn't make the decision."

"She didn't stop them," Martin said, and stared straight ahead, pausing, as if gathering the sound from around the room.

"When did you leave the rehab place in Vermont?"

"A couple of days ago."

"They just let you go?"

"Yeah," Martin said experimentally, ignoring whatever rebuttal Brendan might be thinking of offering. After a long journey, arrival felt like a victory.

Norah turned to Brendan. "You're okay with this?"

"He was beginning to get a little restless at the Dunes."

"Restless?"

"Yeah, well, agitated."

"I wasn't agitated, I was *better.* They're just not used to seeing people recover."

Norah watched her father and then looked at Brendan, her head toggling between the two. "You two look *so* much alike."

"Do you think?" Brendan said, looking at his brother, whose face seemed narrow and slightly avian to him. Brendan inadvertently touched his own chin.

"I can't get over it," Norah said.

"We *are* related, after all; that might go some ways to explaining a similarity," Martin said.

Norah ignored her father, turning to Brendan. "Are you up here for long?"

"No plans to leave just yet. We'll see how your dad does."

"Are you still working?"

"No. I retired last year."

"What did you do?"

"I was a veterinarian."

"Do you miss it?"

"Sure."

"Then why did you retire?"

Brendan laughed. "Are you making a documentary now? I was bought out. I had a clinic, and we did well, and so we had a chain of clinics and we were taken over by a fairly big corporation." Martin looked out at his brother, as though he were listening for the first time. "I worked as an employee vet for a couple of years and then it was just time to retire. The practice part was always fun, but in the last few years, before the buyout, I was getting more involved in the business aspects of it. Developing new programs."

"Programs? What, like yoga for cats? The wallet biopsy?" Martin snorted, and Norah shushed her father.

"I developed a program called 'The Canine Continuum,'" Brendan said, and Norah turned to him. "We found out that when a client had to put down an animal, there was a fifty-eight percent chance that person would be 'on hiatus' from the practice for the next year."

"Grieving?"

"Yeah, or for a number of other reasons. And if the client was away for more than a year, there was a further sixty-one percent chance we would lose him or her to another practice altogether. So we would encourage clients to have several animals, you know, offer discounts, so that we would always have them 'in practice.' But people with single animals, that was a challenge, so I developed a program that clients could sign up for where they would never be on hiatus."

"So you'd fix them up with a dog right away?"

"Yeah. They could prebuy; it even turned out to be good business for us to finance the pet ourselves in most cases. But it was more complicated; after a few months, we found that for the client to be completely satisfied, we had to, well, ceremonially recognize the event, you know, the death of one animal, the acceptance of the other." Martin was listening now—with a smirk. Norah looked like she wanted to grab a notebook. "We would arrange for the euthanasia to occur in our grieving room. That's fairly standard veterinary practice, but we would lower the lights and put on some preselected music, and when the client's animal was euthanized, we'd remove it from the darkened room and bring the new animal in. A new puppy or a rescued animal. Whatever. We'd slowly turn up the lights. The person would be with his new dog."

There was a pause, long and deep enough for a loon to have interjected its night call.

"And people like this?"

"People *love* this."

"That's retailing at its creepiest," Martin said.

"It's interesting," added Norah.

"It was like discovering electricity. Our one-year hiatus rate decreased to six percent. Overall, three-year retention of clients is now at ninety-three percent. It was a revolution in small-animal practice. No downside: improved retention *and* client satisfaction, plus we were placing animals from rescue organizations."

"What sort of music do people choose?"

"What?"

"Do people get to choose their music during this whole 'continuum' thing?"

"Sure."

"What do they listen to?"

"People bring in their own music, sometimes. And if they don't have music with them, we have a wide selection. Some New Age stuff, ambient music. And, you know, ballads. That song from the movie *Titanic.*"

Martin and Norah nodded and the conversation halted, ebbing into remembered music and the sound of eating, broken only when Martin accidentally swept a fork off the table. Brendan got up to retrieve it, but in one movement Martin swooped down and plucked it off the floor with his right hand, the speed leaving Brendan in mid-reach, open-handed. Norah noticed.

"You seem to be doing pretty well, Dad."

"I told you. I keep telling everyone. In some ways, you know, I feel better than before. Clearer."

"When I saw you in March, before you went to that rehab place in Vermont—you were still in the hospital, I think—no one thought you'd walk again."

Martin sat forward. "Who didn't think I'd walk?"

"What?"

"Who, specifically?

"Well, just everyone. The doctors. Mom spoke to the doctors. . . ."

"What about Jean-Sebastien and Catherine?"

"I didn't speak to them."

"Did I tell you I was heading up here?"

"Martin, give it a rest," Brendan said.

"Let me finish. Did I call you or tell you I was coming up here?"

"Tonight?"

"Not tonight. In February, before I was injured."

"No."

Brendan watched his brother wheel around to face him, his gaze indiscriminate, spraying the room with unfocused anger. Refrigerator, brother, window.

"You see?"

"But you never tell me where you're going, Dad."

"That's not the point. If I was doing something so out of the ordinary, I think I would have told someone."

Norah looked at Brendan.

"He doesn't think it was an accident. He thinks someone deliberately injured him."

"I thought it was some guy in a truck," she said.

"Yeah, yeah. But someone got me out on the road that night."

"So that you'd get into an accident?"

"I'm sure of it. There's no way I should have been out there."

"And you don't remember any of it?"

"Pieces. Moments around Christmas. I remember speaking to your mother."

"It could have been just an accident," Brendan repeated.

"Convenient, though, wasn't it? I'm pushed out, my plan for the consulate project completely abandoned, and then, this accident."

"You walked away from the project, Martin."

"I can't believe that," Martin said. "I would have figured out some way of staying on the project, negotiated something with J-S and Catherine as a consultant, not something in the agreement, but a handshake deal. I'm sure of it. I wouldn't have just taken the money and left."

"Let's talk about something else," Brendan said hopefully, hopelessly, looking over at Norah. Martin didn't move; his right thumb and forefinger pinched the edge of his plate.

"The Sydney Opera House," Martin said suddenly, a non sequitur that froze both Brendan and Norah as they cleared the table. "Utzon, the original architect of the opera house, never saw the completed structure. He resigned from the project halfway through because of arguments about design and cost. Yet he maintained contact with the project. In the end, it was his design. His vision."

Norah gently removed the plate from her father's hand. "Did you explain to your partners that you still wanted to be a part of the project?"

"I proposed a role as a consultant to J-S."

"And what did he say?"

"He said no. If we had agreed to anything before, he's not letting on. That's why they had my license taken away. No license, no role. Convenient."

Norah sensed the topic needed to be changed. "So what are you going to do up here?"

"Get better."

"He has appointments in a couple of weeks at a rehab center back in the city," Brendan interjected. "And it's your grandma's birthday in a few days, so I thought we might make a side trip to Detroit."

"I'm not going to Detroit."

"We'll think about it."

"Mom won't know I'm not there."

"I'll know," Brendan replied.

Martin turned to Norah. "Well, I'm staying. I have a ton of

work to do. Given what's happened, what with the accident and everything, I need to keep busy. Keep my name in the public eye."

"Do you have other projects?"

"I'm thinking about an article on Melnikov. Maybe a biography."

"Oh yeah, the guy you told me about, the cylindrical house, right?" The way Norah said it, Brendan felt she could have simply raised an index finger to her head and made a circling motion. Martin seemed to sense it, too.

"Yes, Norah. The guy in the *house.*"

"He had me bring along a trunkload of notes," Brendan added, "and that model, too. Is that his house?"

"No, that's something else. His house was different."

"Cylindrical. *Very* cylindrical, as I recall," Norah explained to Brendan, and then turned to her father. "Who are you writing it for?"

"I don't know just yet. Maybe it'll be a book."

"That's amazing, Dad. Last time I saw you, you couldn't read."

"Well, that's still hard for me. Writing is still difficult, too, and I end up doing most of it from memory. It's an odd feeling, I've been trying to put the story together, a Melnikov biography, but it's just sort of stuttering along. And yet I feel like it's there. Waiting for me."

Brendan started on the dishes, pulling them clean from a sinkful of soapy water. Norah stood beside him, drying dishes while Martin sat silently behind them.

"How long have you been doing documentaries?"

Norah glanced over her shoulder at Martin in a way that could only be called *wryly.* Martin, perhaps thinking Melnikov thoughts, didn't return her glance.

"I've only started documentary work recently. I did informational films before. Training films for corporations."

Martin piped up. "You could have used her for your dog-killing thing."

"Right fucking charmer, isn't he?" Brendan whispered.

"I'm going to sit down in the living room." Martin announced, and stood up. Norah and Brendan turned around to watch his wobbly first steps become steadier. This is his house, something he created. Maybe he will do okay here, Brendan thought.

"My stuff is in there," Norah said to her father.

"That's okay. I won't touch it." Martin's voice echoed slightly.

Norah and Brendan quietly continued with the dishes. The sink of suds and the gurgle of dishes as they were submerged were hypnotic. Brendan felt it was almost a shame to interrupt it.

"But you're working on something now?" Brendan asked.

"Editing."

"I'd love to see it."

"It's pretty rough, but sure."

With Martin reclined on the couch, Norah opened her laptop and pushed it back on the coffee table so that they all could see it. She guided them through the footage, which at first looked like a group of explorers clambering through a cave. But as the camera moved back, you could see that they were not in a cave, but emerging though the rubble of what was probably a tunnel into the more orderly wreckage of a larger underground chamber. There were three in the group—two men and a woman—all disappearing in darkness or suddenly caught in the glow of the camera lights. They wore harnesses and headgear and moved around one another in a way that Brendan could tell suggested complete familiarity. Brendan looked at his brother, squinting at the monitor. Martin sat forward, as well.

"They're exploring," Brendan said, looking to Norah for her to correct him. She simply nodded.

"It's dark," Martin added. "Who are these people?"

"Brendan's right. They're explorers," Norah said. "They call these 'urban expeditions.' They find abandoned buildings and enter them and then record what they see."

"Trespassing," Martin murmured. "They could get themselves killed. Do you film them vandalizing things, too?"

"They don't disturb anything. They record," Norah said in a way that Brendan knew had been practiced, perhaps just for this moment.

On the monitor, the group had entered a long passage rimmed by the masonry of another era. No missing bricks, the mortar as solid as the earth itself, all unchanged after a hundred years. And yet unused, meaningless. Brendan wondered whether the sight of their work would please the builders or leave them in despair. Maybe they would be indifferent.

"Where are they now?"

"This is an abandoned subway station in Toronto, Dundas."

"I didn't know they had abandoned stations there," Martin said.

"Not many people do. But it's there, under the ground."

"Well, I've never heard of it," Martin said, and sat back.

Norah smiled. "So that means what? It doesn't exist?"

"No. No. It's just I'm surprised to hear about this."

"Stations like this are pretty common. New York has a whole line of abandoned subway stations, but they've been sealed off by security since 9/11."

Brendan sat forward. "These people would have a field day in Detroit. The whole downtown is like this."

"Detroit is like Machu Picchu to this community. . . ."

"This *community*? There's a community? "Martin said, laughing.

Norah ignored her father. "They were heading to Detroit the last time I spoke with them.

"Detroit is a disgrace," Martin volunteered.

"Oh yeah? When was the last time you were back?" Brendan asked.

"The funeral. Are you saying it's not a disgrace?"

"Detroit is complicated," Brendan said. "Thirty years without visiting is a bit long to offer an opinion. And *disgrace* is a strong word."

"*Disgrace* is the right word. You remember the Central Station; you remember what Detroit let happen to that? *That* is a disgrace." He turned to Norah, hoping to make his case more persuasively. "Huge building, beautifully appointed. A main concourse that would rival any station in the country."

"Is it still open?" Norah asked.

"It closed in 1968," Brendan told her.

"Torn down?"

"Still standing," Martin added. "One big vandalized shed."

"They might turn it into a central police station," Brendan said in a tone that he recognized was common among former residents when describing plans in Detroit. It was almost a Detroit dialect: part yearning, part resignation, so instantly recognizable to the brothers that neither had to say that the plan was unlikely.

Norah picked up a small remote and advanced the video to another point, where the three explorers stood frozen. She pressed PLAY and one of the men lifted his hand to the camera and smiled. *Hi Norah.*

"Who's that?" Martin asked.

Norah frowned performatively. "Stefan."

"These people know you?"

"I've gotten to know them. I spent six weeks with them."

"Going into these places? You know, places like this aren't just abandoned; they're condemned. They're fenced off for a reason; the support structures are unsound, the air is unsafe. . . ."

"I know that."

"You obviously don't." Martin shook his head.

"I'm making a documentary about these people. I just can't just back away the moment . . ."

"I don't see the reason you're following them in the first place."

"They're interested in these spaces, these great spaces, hidden away."

"They're trespassers."

"Matta-Clark was a trespasser."

"That's different. He had architectural training; he knew what he was getting into."

"So it's okay to do this as long as you're part of a club."

"Who's Matta-Clark?" Brendan asked, not taking his eyes off the screen, watching how the camera lingered on Stefan, big-shouldered and smiling, reminding him of Paul, his youngest. He wondered what cellular coverage was like out here.

"It's not a club. But it takes specialized technical training to know that the floor won't collapse under you."

Norah turned to Brendan. "Matta-Clark was a performance artist who worked with buildings. He sawed a house in half and cut holes in warehouse walls."

"Matta-Clark was an architect," Martin interjected.

"And what, exactly, did he build?" Norah asked.

Martin shrugged. "Granted, he built nothing. Lots of people call themselves filmmakers without ever having shown a film."

Norah pointed the remote at her computer and the image of Stefan ducking under a concrete beam blinked away to blackness.

"I'm sorry," Martin said. Norah said nothing, closing the laptop before standing up and heading for the door, leaving Brendan staring straight ahead. Martin sat back in his chair, his glasses obscuring whatever he was looking at. "I'm sorry," he repeated. Brendan wasn't certain whether Martin knew his daughter was gone. "I'm sorry."

Once he had helped Martin into bed and finished dispensing the medication, Brendan settled into his own room. He checked his phone for a signal and, surprised at how good it was, checked his voice mail, to find it empty. It would be early evening in Portland and he imagined his sons cleaning up from the day's business. The remains of the day: oil in the fryers and sore muscles and the warmth of a used kitchen. Occasionally, he fantasized about just showing up unannounced on some Portland sidewalk, sidling up to La Cucina della Puccio and ordering some arancini. The fantasy ends uncomfortably when the order is handed to him without any acknowledgment of who he is from the two young men inside, who are perhaps just too busy to recognize their father on the other side of the window. Rita had been the one to support them in their idea for a food truck. He'd been the one, with all his business savvy, to throw cold water on the proposal, saying that a life as an executive chef in a restaurant was a safer way to start out than a crazy money pit of a food truck. The thought of finishing that order of arancini and just standing there on a wet Portland pavement, the pause and the silence after the last taste, and what the silence meant, was what kept him from pursuing the idea. Brendan looked away from his phone. From his room, he could see down to the patio, where Norah had returned, now reclined on a lounge chair. A small orange star glowed in the darkness beside her.

When he opened the door to the patio, she jerked her head and reflexively pulled the joint away, cupping it in the hand farthest away from him. A reflex, one he'd seen in his own kids, triggered by sudden parental appearance.

"Do you mind if I hang out here?"

"No. No. It's just you, right?"

"He's asleep."

She craned her neck, seeking the verification of the empty patio door behind him.

"Has he been paranoid like this?"

"This? This is good day for him. You should have seen him when he went in to confront people at work." Norah was nodding slowly, as though lapping up something whose taste she was already familiar with. "It didn't go well."

"Susan told me. The whole buyout thing was a major shit storm at the firm. Lots of lawyers. My dad didn't go easily."

"I only saw the lawyers' letters. Of course, he doesn't remember agreeing to the buyout. I had to explain everything to him when I went through his mail, and he didn't deal with it any better the second time around."

"Susan said that it was a number of things—there were problems with the consulate project and he was taking the blame for that. He was—what's the polite word? Uncompromising. And I think there were other disagreements. Business stuff. This was a business decision, Susan told me."

"She stayed."

"She did," Norah said.

Brendan walked up to the edge of the patio, putting both hands on the railing. He tried to look past the modest haze of the patio lights to where the night's blackness hung heavily.

"He doesn't mean a lot of what he says."

When he turned around, he found Norah just looking at him. "Did my mom ask you to say that?"

"No."

"He gets me uptight."

"He's good at it."

He caught himself looking at her hand, watching a single line of smoke rise and then twin before dissolving from signal to noise. His attention was obvious even to her.

"You want some?" she asked.

"No, thanks," Brendan said, waving her off, one swipe of a gesture vigorous enough to disperse the smoke, whose smell he already recognized was calling out to him in a deep, neurochemical way. "I'm fine. I go to AA for some issues I had," he continued, to which Norah stubbed out the joint.

"Sorry."

"No, it's good now. I'm good."

"Was it booze?" she asked, surprised.

"Uh, everything, really. Booze, pot, pills. You name it. In the end, it's always about behavior anyway."

"Was it because of Vietnam?"

"No. I don't think so. Did your father tell you that?"

She shook her head. "He doesn't talk much about before. I just knew you'd been there."

"It wasn't the war. I had some problems over the last couple of years. "

Norah looked at him in that way that made him want to tell her more, an urge he was relieved he could control.

"Do you want to sit down?"

"Sure." Brendan lifted his leg over one of the lounge chairs, straddling it for an uncomfortable moment before sitting down. "He's messed up after this accident."

"I can tell."

"He's lost everything and he's blaming."

"My father has his limitations, you know. He had them before the accident."

"It's just that everything has been taken away from him."

"Well, you're here. Susan's around. I'm around."

"He needs something more than us."

"That, in a sentence, is my father's problem."

"I know, I know, but I think he'd really benefit from a gesture, you know, something to help him get back his confidence."

"I don't know if confidence is the problem."

"I think he's afraid. Look, I hope you don't think I reduce everything to animal behavior, but this is fear aggression. All I'm saying is that if we help him feel that confidence about his life, it could help. . . ."

"You mean like helping him to get his license back?'

Brendan shook his head. "No, I think that's impossible. But I was thinking about this house. He built it. In a way, it's a statement, personally and professionally. He needed to come back here, I think, for a reason." Norah nodded, looking like she'd regretted prematurely darkening the ashtray. "I thought that you could offer to do a short film about him and this house." He lifted his hands as if to acknowledge the wary look she deployed. "No. Hear me out."

She was shaking her head, "It's self-serving, Brendan. And maudlin. God, he'd never agree."

"I think he would. I'm not asking you to turn this into a project, but the process would be important to him. It's a way you could relate to each other differently—you know, as professionals. And it would take his mind off . . . well, everything."

Norah was silent. He imagined her trying in vain to muster the counterargument, how the pros and cons would resist being weighed in the soft chemical buzz and the cricket song and the lakeside darkness. How it would be just a well-meaning request from a smiling long-lost uncle. And as Brendan waited for her answer, he tried not to feel shame, but he was glad it was dark on the patio and that the details of their conversation, beyond what he could get her to agree to, would likely be forgotten.

Chapter 13

The sound of Norah's voice on the other side of his bedroom door surprised Martin. It was late, and for a moment he wasn't even certain that he had heard her, but then she repeated herself. Norah's voice behind the door. Soft and so unusual. Susan, well, that would have been a different story; she would have been banging on the door like a cop with a warrant, eager to rejoin whatever argument had been left unresolved. But Norah was different; a girl who retreated into silences that had often made him regret what he'd thought was a harmless tone of voice or particular choice of word. Sharon was the one who understood this truth about their younger daughter, who would invariably coax Norah into explaining the reason for her upset with her father and then prompt him with the apology. When she explained that she wanted to make a short film about him, he was uncertain what she meant. He thought at first that she wanted to make the film about his recovery, and his first impulse was to say no, shuddering at the thought of that difficult trajectory back to the Dunes and the abyss that had preceded it. She pulled a chair up to his bed, and for a moment she looked at the model of Melnikov's pavilion, which sat on the nearby desk, and he could not help but see this as a gesture to get him to acquiesce, to agree in some fundamental way to be just another subject.

But she explained that she wanted to make a film about the lake house. It was, she said, his most important work, his most personal, and she wanted use it as a starting point: to walk around with him, ask a few questions about how he'd started his career and what he thought about architecture now. Now. Now that he wasn't able to practice anymore. She wanted to film this, she said. It caught him by surprise, for he could not remember her ever having taken such an interest in his opinions. It would only require him to spend an afternoon filming, Norah said, leaning in as she spoke to him. He tried to focus on her.

"Why are you interested in this?"

"I suppose I've never asked you," she replied.

No ulterior motive. A disinterested observer. He hadn't considered her in this way, considered her curiosity. She had always been the less outgoing of his daughters, the one resistant to his suggestions about considering interior design (he got an earful from Sharon about that, about not giving Norah space). After college, she had drifted through a series of jobs, and he had dutifully stopped asking her about what was happening, Sharon's *space* admonition recurred in his mind each time they met, and over the years he had resigned himself to her eventual low-level harmlessness, even uselessness. She'd disappeared. How could that have happened? It had all come at an incredibly busy time; the preliminary work for the consulate competition was just beginning and they had cut the ribbon on the archives building in Edmonton. He had felt a twinge of embarrassment when he learned she was enrolled in film studies, the unease arising not from the subject material Norah had chosen but from the fact she was already well into her second semester when he found out, inadvertently, from Susan. She hadn't asked him for his advice or his money. Maybe this was her way of showing him the seriousness of her plans, he thought.

It also occurred to him that a short film could be the way for him to stay in the public eye, the one venue available to him to maintain an association with his vision of what the consulate could have been. Who knew where something like this would be broadcast—in fact, it wouldn't even need to be broadcast; maybe it would just go viral and he would become a cause célèbre, making his case to the public and contesting the suspension of his license. He could turn the opening of the consulate into a moment of high drama; Martin versus Catherine and J-S and the Russians, one man against the system, show them for the opportunists they so clearly were. His plans for the consulate side by side with what the eventual designs would be. The visionary in contrast with the compromised.

"Sure, I'll do it."

"Are you up for it tomorrow?"

"Yeah, I'll be ready," he said, and he was fairly certain Norah smiled.

She closed the door as he said "Thank you." He lay back in bed, trying to organize some sort of monologue for Norah's film. A manifesto would be wrong, too strident. He needed to talk about his history, his influences. The first thoughts that came to him were reflexively about Melnikov, the house that he'd built, and for a moment he had trouble sorting through the facts, pulling threads of now-intertwined stories apart.

Now he knew why he had made Brendan take him out to the lake: It was intuitive. We seek what we need, he thought, and this house was unmistakably, immutably *him.* There was a point in each project where you would necessarily have to walk away, but this house was different. He stood from his bed and put both hands on the base of the window, staring out into the darkness of the lake.

He knew the land from when there was nothing here. He had walked the property with Sharon and her parents the summer after they married, the summer they'd decided not to abandon Montreal for Toronto, refraining from joining a more vocal but smaller-scale exodus than the one he'd witnessed growing up in Detroit.

Thirty years before, not fifty yards from the window where he now stood, Martin had declared to his father-in-law that he would design it himself, build it himself. He'd watched the corners of Henry's mouth turn up fifteen degrees (maybe Henry had known, even then, how the zoning headaches, the Lac Massawippi Residents Association's objections and injunctions would follow such a boast, how all of that would end up emboldening such a plan).

The four of them had stood there, digesting what he had just said. Shoreline and the thin strip of pine across Lac Massawippi and the perfect marbled corridor of sunlight on the water. He would build a house here. He would make this his. Theirs.

The construction of the lake house was delayed for a year as the Residents Association mulled the possibility of a postmodern addition to the Lac Massawippi shoreline community of, as they explained in their first letter, "more aesthetically consistent" cottages. There were meetings to explain the association's concept of aesthetic consistency, hoping the young architect in question would understand the concerns of the community and revise his plans. An impasse followed, lawyers' letters were exchanged, and a zoning board arbitration hearing was scheduled.

The saving grace for the lake house was that the galvanized metal facade that had been so widely maligned and served the source of the complaint (Martin had received anonymous hate mail that he, like any self-respecting architect, carried around in his breast pocket like a threat from a rival suitor) was essentially hidden from view by the foliage and the local geography, and the "less offensive" glass wall that made up the western—waterfront—elevation was really the public face of the building. And if Martin Fallon wanted to indulge his architectural fancy, as the Residents Association grudgingly admitted once the arbitrator's decision has fallen against them, they had no recourse to stop him.

He built the lake house for himself and his family, according to his exact specifications, and in his life Martin admitted experiencing no greater professional satisfaction than watching the lake house take shape on the shoreline. Yes, the lake house was the vital thing, he told himself, source material.

Martin returned to bed, closed his eyes, and could see again the tradesmen arriving, the successive arrival of pickup trucks, and it was during this thought that the action sped up, night and day strobing, the foliage of the property's trees swelling and falling like his own breath, the structure beginning to emerge from the ground. Existing. He remembered the trailer that they'd brought to the site that summer, the tiny space that they'd all crammed into for three weeks, and he remembered silently and slowly making love with Sharon in the dark of the trailer, their girls sleeping mere feet away, and he thought that nothing was claustrophobic if it was truly desired, and these were our desired lives.

Chapter 14

Martin sat very still as Norah prowled the back patio with her camera. Establishing shots, she said offhandedly when he asked what she was doing. *Perspective.* The work before the work. The camera was smaller than Martin had thought it would be, a fragile, almost marsupial presence that settled in her hand. Brendan, standing on the patio with both hands in his pockets, studied the microphone that jutted out of the camera and looked vaguely hurt that he had nothing to do.

"We'll start in a few minutes, Dad," Norah said.

"What are you going to ask me about?" Martin asked, and tried to suppress a yawn.

"I don't typically let people know the questions ahead of time. You okay?"

"Didn't sleep well. What are you going to ask me?"

"How about Melnikov? How far are you on your project about him?"

"It's coming along," Martin replied, lying. "Bit by bit. I'm trying to dictate, and that makes it slow going. But it feels ready, you know?"

"Know the feeling well. Let's see, then; we can talk basics. Early influences. We can discuss the house itself later," Norah said, pointing the camera at the house and walking away from him, with Brendan in tow. "We'll start in a couple of minutes, Dad."

His career—his life, really, when he thought about it—began long before he found himself roaming around Melnikov's backyard with his architecture professor. It started with a walk up a flight of stairs to a second-story architecture office before he was even certain that architecture would be his career. He could still feel that wrought-iron rail under his right hand. It was Montreal in the autumn of 1968. The city was different without his family, promise and threat both amplified. His first year in Montreal was a year of scraping; a rushed registration at McGill in the faculty of arts followed a frenzied search for a job and a place to live. Eventually, he installed himself in a Park Extension studio apartment with little more in the way of space than a jail cell. The part-time job proved just as unpromising, probably nothing more than gofer work in a small local architectural firm, whose phone number he had torn from the bulletin-board notice pinned up at the School of Architecture. Tolerable and dull, he thought, as he climbed the stairs to the second-story office on Greene Avenue, no more than a block from the sleek new Mies van der Rohe complex that had gone up the previous year. He tried not to think about that; because whatever ambitions he had were tempered by the need for rent money, the need to stay afloat on all accounts. And so, appreciative of dullness and tolerability, he knocked on the door marked EVANS & SMITH—ARCHITECTS already resigned to not having much choice in the matter.

During the interview, Martin thought he picked up on the origins of a frown on Michael Evans's face when he described the circumstances surrounding his flight from Detroit. But Smith, perhaps the younger of the two (by mere minutes, he imagined, as he could almost immediately see them fraternally twinned in the womb, their understanding of limited space and the needs of the other each formed at so early an age) could not suppress his grin at the frisson of giving refuge to a draft dodger. They shook hands. That's how business was done here.

Walker Smith and Michael Evans were old school, bow-tied, tweed-jacketed exemplars of gentlemen architects. *Very Westmount,* he was told—whatever that meant—and only too happy to occupy themselves with midsize projects that seemed forgotten in the glamour of the recent blitz of building in Montreal. Their office—modest, busy, and daily cast into the shadow path of the neighboring Mies leviathans—described their practice very well. The darkness of a modern eclipse in the midafternoon, followed by their inevitable emergence, another day's work fully done.

Evans & Smith were proud generalists, employing no landscape architects ("I rather like that work," Michael Evans said, almost apologetically, to Martin in explanation) and refusing the projects so big that the structural engineering and construction management were beyond them. For Evans & Smith, Martin would answer the phone and organize files and stay out of the way of the real secretary, Simone. In his spare time, he was left alone to, in the words of Walker Smith, do the important work of drafting and thinking without a particular project in mind.

Within a few months, after proving himself generally competent and interested, Martin found himself being invited on site visits with his bosses. What struck Martin most was the silence of the two men as they walked through a site, whether it was the foundation of a project in progress, the empty shell of something they were refitting, or just terrain; the two would not exchange a word. At first, this was disconcerting, leaving him to think he had stepped into the perilous terrain of some fresh spat with an unknowable history, but he soon realized that each was simply working in his own way. Evans would stop to make notes every minute or so while Smith scouted out the periphery of the site.

They would meet back at some point and share a haiku of distilled professional experience, something that, to his untrained ear, sounded only obvious or inconsequential.

"That entrance does not work." The other would nod and make a note.

Martin remembered following a few paces behind his bosses on these visits, not because he was aware of some unspoken rank or out of mute-lackey deference, but simply due to the clumsiness of walking weighed down by the cardboard tubes that held the fine plans of Evans & Smith. He would walk behind them because that was how one observed them best. This was where he decided on a life in architecture.

Along with his papers attesting to his landed immigrant status, his only other belongings on arrival in Montreal were two suitcases, in one a portfolio of the sketches and renderings he had made in the expectation that he would eventually apply to American schools, growing now thanks to spare moments and materials courtesy of Evans & Smith. The sum of his work. The fear and exhilaration of having only that, of arriving someplace with nothing more than that. Outside his nearest neighbors and the two architects who employed him, Martin couldn't remember speaking to anyone that first year, as if to reinforce that idea of himself as a true refugee, burying himself in course work that would allow him to be accepted to the School of Architecture.

When he received the letter notifying him that he'd been officially accepted to the School of Architecture, he told only Smith and Evans. They'd both written letters on his behalf, vouching for him in that hopeful, unreserved way that a referee can only do for someone he doesn't completely know. And besides, these two men were the only people he knew personally. At a celebratory dinner they held for him—attended by their wives and Michael Evans's young niece, Sharon, who was in town from Toronto for medical school interviews at McGill—Martin remembered how Michael Evans had given him a friendly warning about the amount of work demanded of an architecture student. "Worse than medical school," Walker Smith added, winking at Sharon across the table. And Martin nodded avidly at this, not just accepting but also welcoming another immersion, another potential layer of work between Detroit and himself.

At the end of that night, Michael Evans offered to drive him home, and Martin recalled that moment, being in the backseat next to Sharon. He remembered her face and its fresh mystery, but for a moment it was Norah's face from just minutes before. But what he recalled without confusion was that she wore a yellow sundress. He remembered this color on Sharon as it repeatedly honeyed and darkened and then burst again, a small celestial event precessing there next to him, over and over, as the car passed through the shadows cast by the streetlights.

Martin had been embarrassed by the sight of his apartment building and so asked Michael Evans to drop him off at a more respectable corner in Park Ex, a few blocks from where he lived. Evans told him to get a good night's sleep and then come to the office the next day ready to work. He got out of his car and shook Martin's hand again. From the curb, he waved good night, and as the car turned the corner, the last thing Martin saw was Sharon's face in the window, glancing back. He saw this. This happened. He was sure of it.

Without them, he would be nothing. Have nothing. It was this thought, Martin realized, that had tugged at him early that morning in bed as he awoke with thoughts of what Norah would ask him. He would mention Evans & Smith to Norah and then stop, all the firm's contributions to his life ending with nothing more than a punctuation mark. Or he would say nothing at all.

Martin reasoned that it had taken him no more than a semester in architecture school to abandon his regard for Evans & Smith and their quaint habit of building things, to become a devotee of André Lanctot, the professor who would introduce him to early modernism and the works of Melnikov and the Soviet Constructivists. Lanctot was an architectural theorist and resident brooding visionary on the faculty, an altogether more fitting mentor for an aspiring student. And, as is the case with any hero, Lanctot's potential fault of never actually having built anything was reconfigured by his protégé into a virtue: He regarded Lanctot as someone whose thoughts and ideas were rigorous enough to exist independently of a mere structure.

Evans & Smith had been so completely forgotten that by the time of his first real date with Sharon—made following a chance meeting at the campus bookstore eighteen months after their introduction—that the only subject he was interested in talking about was Lanctot: the new monograph on the Soviet Constructivists, the plan to go to Moscow to photograph Melnikov's house, how he was hoping to be the one student chosen to go along. He remembered that Sharon seemed to be unimpressed and how she teasingly asked why he thought Lanctot was so special—he didn't, after all, *build* things—and Martin remembered stumbling as he tried to relate how Lanctot caused him to see buildings differently, how his value lay outside the mere physical artifacts that an architect left behind. *The mere physical artifacts that an architect left behind,* He cringed as he remembered having said that to Michael Smith's niece and marveled at Sharon's composure for not abandoning the table for a less idiotic dinner companion. In this memory, Sharon wears a yellow dress, a conflated moment that makes him nervous that all his memories, even the most vivid and meaningful, are not facts, but creations to serve some need he cannot admit or fathom.

"Tell me about your influences, then," Norah said, and for a moment Martin felt blinded by the late-morning sun.

"I was fortunate to have studied under and been a protégé of André Lanctot, who fostered my interest in the Soviet Constructivists in general and Konstantin Melnikov in particular, and, well, he was key in both helping shape any aesthetic I have tried to establish as well as developing my own writing about the period."

"Was Lanctot responsible for any notable works?"

"Professor Lanctot was an architectural theorist, perhaps one of the brightest architectural minds this country has produced. He wrote and taught, but he didn't build."

"You visited Moscow with him, saw Melnikov's house, didn't you?

"I did," Martin said, and in saying so was overcome with a feeling—vague but with complete certainty—that he had already spoken about the visit, that it had been discussed and prepared in a way that made talking about it now repetitive. Derivative. "I met him. Once."

"Didn't you also work with Michael Evans?"

The question felt like a thumb had been gently but assertively placed on his breastbone, and Martin tried to look at Norah for the first time during the interview, but he was able to focus only on the gaping mouth of the camera. "Uh, well, yes. I wasn't an architect, or even a student of architecture when I worked with him."

"But you did work with him."

"I did. I worked for him. How did *you* know about Michael Evans?"

Norah tilted her head away from the camera and toward her

father. "Mom told me. He was, after all her uncle. Great-uncle to the filmmaker, if you must know."

"I didn't know she'd ever spoken to you about him. What else did she say about him? About me?"

"She told me that he said you were a better architect before you had ever gone to your first class than most of the new graduates he hired."

Martin nodded and looked out at the lake. It was natural, he thought, for a young man to seek out someone who could make him great, that even Evans knew this and understood this was a necessary step in a young architect's education. It was almost to be expected. And as Martin reassured himself, he also understood that just forgetting Smith and Evans had been somehow insufficient. Adopting Lanctot as a mentor had required something more declarative than simply leaving his former teachers behind. And so, on the day when Lanctot deigned to ask Martin about his work experience, Martin mentioned Evans & Smith and, when his new mentor's face registered only puzzlement at the name, Martin gestured in a way to reassure Lanctot that there was no reason that he should know the name of a small and inconsequential local firm. More than thirty-five years later, Martin remembered the moment and, more vividly, the gesture, a brushing motion with his right hand, as though trying to remove lint from his pant leg. Subtle, succinct, and nothing less than a repudiation.

"That was very kind of him to say. Your mother never told me he said that."

"It was years ago, and I guess she felt it was said in confidence. He also said that he understood why you never came to him for a job after you graduated, that you were as ambitious as you were talented."

Martin felt the corners of his mouth draw tight and wondered whether the camera could register the difference between a grimace and a smile. "It sounds more like a critique than a compliment."

"I don't know how he meant it, Dad."

"Could I ask you a question?" Martin said. There was a pause.

"You're asking *me*?" Norah said.

"Yes," Martin replied. "Turn the camera off."

"What did you want to ask?"

"Turn the camera off. Please." Norah put the camera aside. "Tell me: What do you think he meant?"

Norah paused for a moment. "I don't know. I do think it would be ideal if talent and ambition *were* somehow matched, and maybe that's all he meant; maybe he wished that sort of balance for you. I see filmmakers who have all the talent in the world and no ambition, and I get the feeling it's more of a pity than a tragedy. I suppose it's sad, but it's self-contained. Maybe they'll fail, or maybe they'll create a masterwork that only they will know about. I always found it a little bizarre—people really seem to have a problem with what they see as talent going to waste, like it's a moral failing. Lots of people have ambition to spare, ambition that so completely outstrips their talent, and nobody seems to have a problem with that. And ambition is different, too, I think; it answers different needs. I think I can tell when I'm watching a piece by someone who is more ambitious than talented."

"In what way?"

"Maybe it's just me, but things seem calculated. There's less joy."

Martin sat back in his chair. "What do you think of this house?"

"I think it's fine."

"How would you describe it to someone, a friend, who's never seen it?"

"It doesn't matter what I think."

"It does. You've lived here."

"It's your house, Dad."

"It was meant to be more than that."

"I think of it like sculpture. I think I can appreciate it best in that way."

"As a house. Tell me what you think of it," Martin said. Brendan had reappeared in the outer limits of his field of vision after having momentarily vanished. He had his back turned away from Martin and Norah, as out of earshot as one could be without taking to the water. Martin looked back at his daughter, who seemed to be studying something in her hands before raising her gaze to meet his. "Is there joy in this house?"

Norah smiled in a gentle way and shrugged and said nothing. She looked over her right shoulder, out to the lake.

From inside the doorway darkness of the lake house, Martin listened to the sound of Norah's car first being loaded and then driving off, the fading sound of an engine like an ellipse.

Earlier, after a couple of phone calls, Norah had announced with a sudden urgency that her plans had changed and she needed to leave. As she packed up her belongings in the spare bedroom, Brendan came to him, grabbed him by the arm, and leaned close to him, speaking in reined-in whisper that felt like a hammer tapping an eggshell: "You should say something to her."

"What could I say?"

"You could say anything, that it doesn't matter what she thinks about the house. *About a house,* for God's sake, Martin. She's just upset that you felt insulted."

"I did feel insulted," Martin replied. Brendan's face appeared blank and he let go of his brother.

Martin retired to his room and then returned in silence to the doorway to listen to her say good bye to Brendan. The sound of their voices was replaced by a short *shush* of gravel being disturbed, which he assumed was the moment where his daughter stood on her toes to kiss his brother on the cheek. He listened for, but did not hear, his own name spoken.

Chapter 15

Martin sat motionless under the sun until he felt the unmistakable tingle of a burn on his forearms. He tried not to think about Norah, probably now on the highway, still a couple of hours from Montreal. Whatever direction. Just putting distance between the two of them.

He turned his head away from the sun. It wasn't his habit to spend much time on the patio, and it was a surprise to him to discover that at this time of day the sunlight struck the glass on the curved lakefront side of the house in such a way that it seemed magnified as it hit the patio, producing a discomfort similar to Jean-Sebastien's design flaw in the old F/S+H offices. No one, not Sharon or even Agnetha, had ever mentioned this to him.

He had designed the lake house with one image in mind: at dusk, in deepest summer, lit from inside, and this image, the way he always truly saw the house, brought him joy. In that sense, he had exceeded expectations—his own at least. It was that very image in his mind that Martin remembered now, how the sun dipped behind the pine-forest ziggurats across the lake and the evening took on a glow of latent incandescence. The magic hour: everything quietly, effortlessly stunning. The lake house, newly completed, was gorgeous, cool greens that surprised and yet seemed inevitable. Sharon was next to him, her arm around him as they sat on the patio that night hosting a dinner for the Residents Association members. He remembered the impression he had of these people, fresh from their clapboard cottages and Canadianas and what he assumed were nervous lakefront lives. He told himself several times as the evening got under way that the tone of the evening had to be just right—the last thing this gathering should be was a celebration for having won a zoning battle. It had to be a gesture—conciliatory and at the same time gently justifying—to those who were still not convinced that the right party was victorious.

He could remember so vividly the other women at the party: a cluster of lakeside doyennes and their monumental spouses, the clique of legacy lakesiders who had nothing to prove and ruled from a distance like a well-tanned politburo. This group was offset by another category of female guest, and whether it was new money or fewer than four generations on the lake, these women—only slightly older than Sharon and Martin—struck him as oscillating with the energy of striving for some urgent yet mysterious goal. Their silent, sullen husbands—temporarily exiled from their *centre-ville* fiefdoms and temporarily banned by their wives from the nearest golf course—followed a step behind like cut-rate bodyguards.

Martin considered himself wary of generalizations, but he couldn't help but think of this group of women as a particular subspecies—the wrong word—a superspecies unto themselves: ridiculously well educated, but absented from the working world, unencumbered by the wearying demands and absurdities of daily toil. This freedom showed. They appeared to glide, float, and swivel, as if carried on some invisible mechanism, every sequence of movement a practiced and elegant coiling and uncoiling of a yoga-honed carriage. Anglophone and francophone, they mingled freely, as though it was clear to all that they were above the menial divisions of language. They even stood differently than Sharon, who, in her posture, seemed to carry the burden of cumulative night shifts in the emergency room, of responsibilities not of her own choosing.

He had seen what a mistake it was to underestimate them—away from the lake, they ran their households, kept their power-broker husbands at heel, and fanned out across the city to impose their will on whatever arts or charity group they chose, and with their attentions not divided by work or the day-to-day routines of children, they brought an unnerving focus to their pursuits. One guest mentioned she had begun serving on the board of an art gallery, describing the group dynamics and her fellow board members in such a way that he was certain a bloodless coup was already under way. Another, who had obviously never had to deal personally with the damage a raccoon can do to a house, spearheaded a program to "rescue and repatriate" wild animals, which would no doubt leave them all picking up shredded garbage and skidding on droppings for generations to come. A third, who appeared at his shoulder in a one-piece tennis dress whose shade of red should have been visible to forest rangers in Trois-Rivières, told him in an effortless first sentence of introduction that she was on the Historic Buildings Committee for the city of Montreal and mentioned the dean of architecture by his childhood nickname. Martin nodded politely, all the while admitting to, and reviewing in his mind the reasons for, a certain disdain for these women. Part of it was a class thing, he thought, an admittedly less than completely fair proletarian sneer at their unabashed wealth and voluntary uselessness, but most of his antipathy came from firsthand knowledge of having had to deal with their never-ending demands as clients and coming to understand that the grief they brought to those whose services they retained was rarely worth the commission.

But this night brought a revelation: Tonight, these women seemed different. Maybe, he thought as he listened to them converse about Lyme disease awareness and Nova Scotia duck tolling retrievers, it was how they seemed to regard his work, the occasional glimpses of softness in their eyes when they looked up at his building. That was the only word for it, *softness.* It was a response that he knew was a sort of resignation, an acknowledgment, and it gave him pleasure in a way that had been, up until that moment, unfamiliar to him. It was an expression that not even Sharon had when she looked at her own house.

He already understood that these women were the tastemakers, and had the design of his house still been disputed, their opinion alone, and their desire to enforce it, would have likely carried the day for him with the Residents Association. Perhaps they had always been his supporters, this thigh-mastered troop of Medicis. His boosters. Standing on the patio with them, he felt the desire to show them the house he had built, to take them inside and walk them through it. The word *squire* came to mind, the verb only slightly more ridiculous than the noun, causing him to pause for a moment until the thought spiraled away like an uncommitted mosquito.

At the end of the evening, Suzanne Desormais, the friend of Dean "Scooter" and co-owner of the small castle up the road from them, put her hand on his shoulder and whispered, *This is visionary.* She asked him for his card and told him that she knew his work, said that she knew whoever built the Kingston Library would come up with something exceptional. He remembered how her fingers had run down the back of his arm from the shoulder to his elbow and although this might all have been inadvertent, he knew at that moment, with a sense that can only be called exhilarated despair, that he would eventually sleep with Suzanne Desormais, that he could already see the inevitable series of events that would include the pretense of a renovation project necessitating a personal consultation, a meeting. With the far end of the lake disappearing in the dusk, he could see it all unfolding, the unraveling of his sense of himself as a trustworthy man and faithful husband: He could see her waiting for him and already appreciated the mechanics of their wordless sex, the experience intensified and simplified by the fact that she wanted nothing more of him than it *be him,* the person who had done what he had done. What he could not foresee, what he would not know until it was over with Suzanne and he had excavated some sort of meaning, aside from the acknowledgment of betrayal and an almost shameful self-contentedness, was what having sex with Suzanne Desormais would evoke in him, that in a conflation of needs his professional work would somehow feel legitimized in extreme sensual pleasure, that he would come to see this woman as his due reward. Meritocratic lust. He remembered looking at Suzanne Desormais at the same moment she touched the inside of his elbow. This is what it would mean to him. He could feel the linear pressure of the tips of her nails against his skin and it only felt inevitable. He thought he could foresee all of this, with Sharon on the other side of the deck with her good mood and tired eyes, and he was uncertain what it would mean to Suzanne Desormais until he realized she has already announced in her codified way what she expected, that he had been commandeered like little more than a capital campaign for lupus research.

Now, the sun at midafternoon bleached the area behind the house into a white and featureless and deeply desiccated landscape. He squinted, effectively closing his eyes against the glare, and finally found the deck, his hands reaching out as he mounted the last of three stairs. The wood of the deck, thick planks of cedar that had been chosen to age into a color that matched the corrugated metal facade, had been replaced in 1994 and again in 2003. They felt almost combustably hot to the touch. Agnetha had wanted to paint them, and when he'd asked what color, truly mystified and eager to know what color could hope to have the same effect as aging wood, she'd replied: "Oh, I don't know; any color would do."

On all fours, he reached out his right hand to try to find something to sit on, anything to get off the planks of cedar, which could not have been any hotter had Agnetha herself painted them in kerosene and set them alight. He thought of how Agnetha would have appreciated him in a moment like this: prostrate, groveling, and, no doubt adding, happy to be so close to the work of his favorite architect! The fingers of his right hand jammed against something metallic, and after shaking the sting out of them, he reached for the object and pulled the wrought-iron leg of a patio chair close to him.

He sat on the chair, pulling his legs up into a lotus position, and faced the lake. The brightness of the sunshine turned the lake water into a sheet of almost unnatural cobalt. Between the lake and the sky, he could find only a small seam of green, the stand of pine across the lake, stitching the scene together. He studied the vista closely and tried to identify the docks of adjacent properties or maybe catch a glimpse of a kayak or canoe, a face he could recognize or the semaphore of a solicited wave, but his vision could not settle on a single familiar marker.

Martin rose from the chair but immediately felt unwell, overmatched by the heat and the effort of maneuvering around the house. He turned around to brace himself against the chair, stooped over with a hand pressed firmly against each armrest. He was able to lift the chair enough that it would move a few inches ahead of him and he repeated this motion, trying not to think of it as a poor substitute for a man who really should be using a walker. In this way, he felt able to go on, satisfied with slow progress, resting after each effort.

Moving closer to the lake, he thought himself able to discern features, but any sustained effort seemed to produce only a distorted image of what he thought he'd remembered so clearly. He was now only a couple of feet away from the edge of the deck; the lake water was now close enough that he was certain he could see the shadows under the small swells kicked up by the wind. He paused, kneeling on the chair, trying to find what was out there in the water, beyond his reach. It was when he began to move his head back and forth, scanning across the lakefront scene, that he caught a glimpse of something that caused him, almost involuntarily, to turn his head farther to the left. The movement itself, the demand to move, felt clumsy and jarring, like the sense of finding only dead space as one stumbled onto the extra step of a darkened basement. But then later, something beautiful and surprising revealed itself to him: a glimpse of the lake that had up to that moment had been hidden, a pulse of something luridly vivid that collapsed in on itself, disappearing when he turned to the right, and then recurring again when he swiveled his head the other way, looking past the limits of what he thought he could see. It was gone. He could not see it. But it was *there.*

Chapter 16

We are not the same, Brendan repeated to himself as he watched his brother approach. The last four months at the Dunes had been given over to his polite acknowledgment of strangers' comments about how they looked alike, how even their gestures bore an uncanny similarity (he was uncertain about what this meant, as Martin's repertoire of gestures for the first two months at the Dunes had been confined to a fairly monotone groaning and pawing at his catheter). And every time Brendan nodded in response to these comments—and he did nod, politely, fraternally—he told himself that they could not be more dissimilar. Just nod, he reminded himself. Nothing more than small talk.

But what struck him as odd was the fact that whenever a person made a comment like this—occasionally staff but usually a family member of another patient at the Dunes—they were invariably smiling. And not just the restrained smile of shared pleasantries among people going through a difficult situation, but that big loopy grin that under any other circumstance would make a person detour around whomever bore such as expression, as it was a fairly reliable marker for an unresolved (but surely soon-to-be manifest) psychiatric disorder or someone perpetrating a sidewalk scam for a couple of dollars.

He had gotten used to nodding, to accepting the little banalities that made the day pass more easily. But he had come to think that even if such expressions were cliché, they were so prevalent that they must have some purpose. A doctor friend of his had told him that there was a sociobiological reason comments about resemblance of a newborn were always directed to the father, that it was thought this was some sort of societal way to strengthen paternal bonding at a crucial moment, reassuring the new parent that the child was indeed his (the assurances of maternity never being necessary to a person who had gone through a pregnancy capped by twenty hours of labor). Maybe the smiles he had been subjected to at the Dunes were nothing more than nervousness in the face of terror and despair and the comments were simply the way that families recognized and reinforced their commitments to their injured kin, that even if their brains had been damaged, they understood, and wanted to know that he understood, that their responsibilities transcended this, that blood was thicker than neurons.

Martin had appeared at the periphery of his vision as a close-to-the-ground hovering presence, which at first he thought was an animal. It was only after he went up to the window and saw his brother straighten up that he recognized him. He watched in some fascination as Martin mounted the steps that led to the patio before crossing the deck as slowly as the shadow of a sundial.

Eventually, Martin commandeered a patio chair, which he would alternately push forward a few inches and then kneel on the seat cushion for five minutes of rest. As he knelt on the chair, Martin stared blankly into the house, in Brendan's general direction, his face pinched into an undecipherable mask.

Anything that they shared was ultimately nothing more than genetic, something completely outside of what either of them wanted to be. Their similarities were the manifestations of random sorting of the same gene pool. For most of their lives they had shared nothing other than this. And yet he liked to think that when he practiced he could recognize animals that had come from the same litter, that even if they had gone to completely different households, he could sense certain aspects of temperament that were shared and outlasted the world's efforts to train them away. But those were the relatively uncomplicated lives of dogs. He could honestly say that he was not like his brother.

Martin moved ever closer to the house, repositioning himself on the chair at an angle to the large central pane of window. From here, he appeared to look into the house at what Brendan assumed must be him. His brother was nothing like him. Brendan approached the window, trying to make out what the hell was going on with Martin now: He was on the other side, a few feet away, perfectly still, sphinxlike, staring through him.

"What do you want?" Brendan said to the pane of glass. To his brother on the other side. There was no answer, not a flicker of response.

His brother just continued staring. Brendan shifted his weight from foot to foot, even swaying slightly to see if his brother's gaze would follow, but it did not. The look on Martin's face reminded him of an animal stare, something that at one time might have caught his eye from deep inside a cage. Quiet incomprehension as the animal slowly awoke from anesthesia, the power of a stare resting solely on its insistence. He liked to think that there was only imperturbable calm behind the eyes of an animal in this state, an equanimity that at one time he'd longed for. But seeing Martin now, he wasn't so sure of this.

"What do you want?" he said again.

Martin slowly extended his legs and took his knees off the chair, seeming to steady himself for a moment before advancing the chair another few inches along its path. He then resumed his perch, his stare. Brendan looked behind him, roughly gauging Martin's line of sight to understand what could be so riveting to his brother, but it was a nondescript path that cut through the large living room and led to the kitchen.

We are not the same, Brendan said to himself, a mantra now as his brother—little more than five feet away—continued to move closer. He looked through the glass at his younger brother and scoffed that anyone could see something in their features that tied them to a common origin. He could keep telling himself that they had turned out to be different men from different countries, strangers really, with nothing in common except for what seemed at that moment to be the increasingly absurd and arbitrary coincidence of a shared last name and childhood address. But of course they shared more, and to watch Martin now, mute and maimed and shuffling along a patio deck, was to remind himself of similar struggle, of the depths that he'd experienced and what appeared to be the unmistakable Fallon penchant for definitive solutions.

Watching his brother, Brendan told himself that it would be best for everyone if he were to extricate himself entirely from this mess, to lay out to Martin everything he knew or assumed and just go home. Let the psychiatrists and the daughters and the exes deal with it. He was not even needed: Martin had ample funds from his disability insurance, an amount no doubt sweetened by the buyout settlement from the partners, a small portion of which would have easily covered the cost of eminently qualified hired care. He imagined the phone book yielding an endless list of professional nurses—and here an archetype, a smiling, patient woman from the Philippines, appeared to him—infinitely more appropriate for the task than he and encumbered by several dozen fewer carousels' worth of personal baggage, someone who would not look at his brother as some slowly approaching menace through the window, whose beatific grace or simple economic need would make her agree to deal with the bag of crazy-ass misanthropy and unresolved issues that were quickly coming to characterize his brother's behavior.

Martin, whose progress had come to a halt about two feet away from the pane of glass, began to rotate his head to the left and then back to the right in a smoothly repetitive movement, which, given his accompanying affectless expression, seemed like a pretty convincing freestyle tai chi move. Trancelike and oblivious, he continued like this for several minutes, the only hitch in the routine was as his head turned to the most leftward position, where he seemed to get stuck, toggling for a second or two, before his head veered away from whatever had caused its moment of hesitation.

Martin's face was frozen, a mask that seemed unreal. Eyes open, but inconsistent with an awake person. Maybe he's had a seizure, Brendan thought, and studied his brother, but he saw no signs of fluttering of eyelids or twitching of muscles, not a speck of froth at the corners of his mouth. It was just Martin's mouth, the edges brought up ever so slightly into a smile, one that reminded an unguarded Brendan of his sons, and, as he caught a glimpse of his own reflection in the massive pane of glass, forced him to admit it was a smile very much like his own.

He curled the fingers of his right hand into a loosely held fist and rapped on the window. His brother startled, orienting toward the sound. "Hey," Brendan said softly, through his own reflection, to his brother outside.

Chapter 17

Martin climbed the stairs to his bedroom and closed the door behind him. The room vibrated with a buzzy energy that felt to Martin like the flickerings of a defective fluorescent light, a dirty little flutter against which even shutting his eyes failed to offer escape. He tried to think of what he'd seen on the back patio before Brendan had interrupted, how for a moment he'd been aware of the lake as somehow starkly different from the way it had appeared before, and he was confused about whether the lake seemed deeper or bluer or more expansive. But it was none of those. It was different in a way that unsettled him. He got out of bed and moved to the window, staring out into the lake to see if it would appear to him that way again. He scanned the shoreline, but nothing happened.

Whatever the change had been, it was one that he could not describe to himself nor even imagine, and so he thought it must have been an illusion or a misperception. It must have been that he'd only believed he'd seen a revelation of something hidden. And yet thinking of what he'd seen in this way seemed untrue. He lay back down on the bed.

The sound of footsteps—not Norah's; how had his first consideration been to assume that she had returned?—arrived in the hallway, then a banging on the door that made Martin start. "You okay in there?" Brendan's voice called out, raised a little. Martin listened to the sound of the mechanism of the doorknob being engaged, slowly, with only enough force, he assumed, for his brother to make sure the door was not locked.

"I'm fine."

Then silence. He was alone. He tried to imagine the bedroom around him and was overcome by the recognition—odd swells of comfort and despair—of the room as a place of retreat. It is natural that I should return here, he thought, and recalled the summer after he'd split up with Sharon, the bruised silences when he decamped to the lake house before finding a place of his own.

And then, though it was not there, Martin remembered the clock on the wall. He remembered the angle of the hands on the clock as he was leaving her on a Friday at quarter past seven in the evening. It wasn't planned that way, or planned to be remembered in that way, but it was simply the time that it had happened. He sees the clock on the wall. He had a bag already packed and in the trunk of his car, but he knew he didn't have everything he needed, and as he began to speak to her over the clearing away the dinner dishes, the thought of what he had forgotten intruded. Static on the airwaves that he could clear. She was wordless. And then she slapped him (the intensity best measured not in the mark it left but by the fact that the sound drew Norah from her eighth-grade homework in an adjacent room). He told himself, as he gathered those things he needed, that he would explain it to the girls later.

He had hoped they would be able to discuss it reasonably. He used the word *rationally.* He wanted to say that they'd become invisible to each other, invisible in that way that was no one's fault, but that simply meant they had evolved into something else. The discussion would have proceeded like that, but she asked him, "Who is it, Martin?" and his argument stalled in some distant place. There was the slap and the silence and the question, always the question, because Sharon knew what any wife knows, what any sentient person who regularly comes into contact with the vagaries of human behavior understands, that no one walked away from something as much as ran toward something. *Who is it, Martin?*

What he could never explain to her was the odd and shameful and unexpected exhilaration of the moment, the arson of a relationship. After years where their bond changed from the unspoken to the invisible to the forgotten, it finally became real again as he told her he was leaving. *I am married to you,* he fully realized as he stood there with his aching face and his declarations of having to go still echoing. *I was married to her.*

This was the place, the house, the room, where Martin understood he was destined to return, where he had come to in those moments in his life when he'd needed reinvention. He was here now, waiting, it seemed, for that moment to occur again, needing that moment to understand the direction his life would take, but all that came to him was the past.

We had become invisible to each other, he repeated to himself. Leaving only meant that we admitted this, that we were truthful. Of course, Sharon was right; she was more truthful than he, even not knowing the full details behind their breakup. There had been a woman, Marina, a designer he'd met on a trip to New York, for whom, in retrospect, he was able to discover only enough emotion to pry himself from his marriage, someone who, in the end, did not even get close enough to slap him. He allowed himself a moment of disappointment (the adult variety: muted, even tinged with relief) when things did not work out, but even with this and the guilt of having hurt Sharon and the girls, he did not question his decision to leave. It was simply what he had to do.

As if to justify his decision, his career entered a renaissance in the years that followed. Jean-Sebastien Houde joined the firm with requisite hoopla and Fallon/St. Joseph became F/S+H, a name initially disliked by Catherine, who read it mathematically and saw herself as relegated to the denominator of the equation with Jean-Sebastien. Success in competitions, a second governor-general for the provincial archive in Alberta, and then a series of projects that Jean-Sebastien called the ICMs—the important cultural monuments: the museum additions and libraries and occasional private prestige residence for whichever tastemaker had wandered into camera range of the local lifestyle magazine.

But that was it. There hadn't been the next step. There had been a steady stream of work, but the name-making projects had not materialized, and as this dawned on him, he realized that the appellation "prominent local architect" was an epithet to his ears, a coded accusation that he had enough talent to make a living and not much more. There would never be a golden season and he would never be great. He realized that if there had been a vision, he had abandoned it, or forgotten it, among all the trappings of security.

Martin looked up at the ceiling of the bedroom and tried to remember the way he'd felt when F/S+H—his design, fought for by him against the wishes of Catherine and J-S—won the competition for the consulate, and it surprised him that it he couldn't recall exhilaration or even vindication, but only the anxiety that came with trying to bring it off.

To be visionary demanded ambition, demanded that one abandon other visions—sometimes visions of security or popular opinion—and he obviously lacked that tenacity. He had conceded to the firm and walked away. The Australian architect Murcutt, whose career could be summed up by saying he had similar ideas to Martin's, except executed on a smaller scale—nothing built outside his adopted country, Australia, just an array of outback cottages that would have barely filled a smallish trailer park—persisted with the material, and what he got for it was the Pritzker in 2002. From vernacular obscurity on the other side of the world to the Pritzker. All it took was perseverance. It had been the one thing that Martin lacked.

The mention of Murcutt's name alone—so phonetically apt, as though describing an inadvertent laceration—was enough to give him pain now, and looking at the man's work, featured everywhere in the aftermath of the Pritzker, his bunk houses and precious sheep-shearing lean-tos, any sense of vindication for the choices he'd once made as a young architect were swallowed in the recriminations he felt for not remaining true to his vision. It could have been him. He had walked away from his family to get to this point, and then just given up.

Melnikov would have persisted, he thought. Melnikov, weathering what he must have thought were the temporary gales of political will and professional envy, would have stayed true. He would have been judged harshly by a man like Melnikov, judged as someone lacking a personal vision or insufficiently principled to follow that vision.

The walls of the room around him seemed to move almost imperceptibly, the insides of an animal breathing along with him.

There were times when Sharon had been so immune to him. Unimpressed that he was an architecture student. At the point where they'd been dating for a year and had discussed moving back together to Toronto when she graduated, he announced that he'd finally been chosen by Lanctot to travel to the USSR—*The USSR! Melnikov! We are going to need visas and diplomatic attachés!* She responded as though he told her he was going to take the bus to Ottawa for the weekend. She been completely unimpressed that he was a draft dodger, maybe even then understanding that escape is escape for any number of reasons, some of them principled, some more plainly pragmatic, some even capricious. She wouldn't sleep with him on that first date, and he attributed this to the fact that he knew her uncle (when he admitted this rationalization later, she snorted a laugh and shook her head, and he didn't pursue it further). Maybe that was why he had fallen in love with her, just the notion that she was different, more discriminating.

And through it all he had believed himself to be a good man, to be the continuing presence as a father to his daughters in spite of the divorce, but he had come to realize, early on, that a distance had been established between them. Norah and Susan would dutifully spend the agreed-upon alternate weekends boarding with him, accompanying him to restaurants or museums with what seemed to be quiet contentment, but he began to realize that an invisible barrier had been erected between them, and no amount of platonic goodwill could make up for the basic fact that he'd walked away from the family. From them. This had been their first betrayal. He accepted this, reasoning that they were almost adults and their new detachment was part of the cost of a difficult decision that he'd had to make. He told himself that this was no reason for him to be upset, that if they did not want to spend time with their father, the mature response would be for him not to insist. He began to find excuses for why he couldn't take the girls on his assigned weekends, and when there came no request, from Sharon or the girls, to make up for the lost days, he understood that a decision had been made.

Within a year, their time together had shrunk to an awkward four days around Christmas and a week at the house at North Hatley, where they seemed to meet only for meals and the wordless appreciation of a sunset, Susan imagining the type of buildings she would want to build, Norah seeking refuge from the house on the patio.

He tried to think of the lake house, how if he were to be judged, it would be by the standard of this work, but he could remember only Sharon and the children, how they'd lived in the camper the summer they set the foundation in North Hatley. How they'd all jumped into the lake the very night they finished the dock, the girls like squealing, barking seals, blue-skinned from the chill of mid-May lake water. The sound of their voices always seemed to form a refrain. A warning that he now felt had gone completely unheeded.

A mild panic, like the sound of water inside a house, arrived, and he got up from the bed and maneuvered to the desk on which the model of Melnikov's pavilion sat. It had been a totem of reassurance, but running his fingers over the surfaces now brought only a feeling of agitation, that the shapes he encountered were not the simple artistic expression of space but had become a barrier to what he needed to know, to what was really there.

Martin closed his eyes and ran his hands along the plane of the desk that the model sat on, for the first time in a while appreciating the grain in the cherrywood, the once-familiar beveled edges. This had been his first desk, a gift from Sharon to him after they were married. After they had refurbished the F/S+H offices and duly filled them with acceptable pieces of modern furniture, the desk looked stodgy and out of place, and so it migrated to a study at home and then, finally, to a bedroom in the country. A typical cascade in the relegation of objects. The desk had been the place where he once kept important papers and plans, but here it had become depersonalized, emptied and mostly unoccupied. Hotel furniture, a surface upon which luggage was placed. Still, it was beautiful, Martin thought, each hand reaching out to grasp a corner of the desk, understanding its heft, its history. A hundred years old, the drawers were a marvel: precision-built and crafted to smoothly glide on nothing more, nothing less, than craftsman's skill. Martin pulled out the center drawer to appreciate this once more. He opened his eyes and found himself staring at a neatly stacked pile of paper, the only thing in the drawer. He picked up the papers and studied the title page. His name beside Melnikov's. Now he remembered.

The Problem of Melnikov: Eight Chapters and One Visit

Martin Fallon

Icons

You paint Mary. Over and over again. Eyes cast down on her folded arms, on her child. Sweet mother, stern mother. You can imagine her face more clearly than your own mother's after a week of painting.

Prokhorov's studio has twenty boys like you, all smelling of tempera, all stumbling toward the same thing, the right expression for the face of a saint. Mary is elusive. Prokhorov spoke to you about your most recent efforts, reining in your desire to depict depth in the painting. He told you there are rules to the painting of icons that must be respected, just as there are rules in any apprenticeship.

You paint Mary.

All you can think about as you paint one more pair of flat Marian eyes is the village of Likhobor, the three-room house where you lived with your family before you were sent here. You can smell the chickens. You can hear your brothers and sisters, even in the silence of the studio.

Prokhorov speaks to you again about your work, the

subtle changes in the facial features of the Virgin, more noticeable with each rendition. Is there a reason for this? You have not noticed, but Prokhorov shakes his head and tells you he has seen this before with the new apprentices. He sits down and talks with you, and this stern man becomes momentarily kind, eyes an icon painter would want to capture for Saint Vladimir.

"Kostia, I will call for your father."

You are alarmed, worried that you have offended your master. But his face remains kindly. He tells you he knows that you wish to return home. It is nothing new with apprentices. You cannot deny he is right. Though you are twelve, you pride yourself on being an adult, and you ask him how he knew you were homesick.

He smiles. "An icon painter must learn to refrain from painting Mary in the image of his mother."

The Particular and the General

At the time, you were just an office boy working in the engineering firm Chaplin established with Zalesskii. *Working* is perhaps the wrong word; the economy this winter has stalled, halting construction in Moscow, and the office is accordingly quiet. Reams of unused paper abound. Your duties are scant and you are left to your own devices. For the first time, you hold a mechanical pencil—itself a miracle of design and utter beauty—and wielding it you experience a precision to drawing that you had never known, a delight no icon could match.

You draw houses and steam engines, intending to take them home and show your brother. But you forget the papers. Vassily, the Ukrainian doorman whose son you resemble, finds the drawings, labels them "Kostia," and puts them on Chaplin's desk. When you are summoned to Chaplin's office, you find the engineer with the drawings held in his hands, and you assume you are to be dismissed for wasting paper.

"Did you draw these?" You nod. Chaplin is silent for some time and you imagine a judgment is being rendered. You are half right. "They're quite good," he says, leafing through the papers.

Your parents, as unfamiliar with Chaplin as they are with the Moscow School of Painting and Sculpture, regard this man's offer of patronage as a somewhat less promising alternative to painting icons. But Chaplin, a self-made man, impresses your father. When you fail your Russian-language examination, Chaplin takes you into his family to benefit from a summer with his daughters' tutor. This, and your eventual acceptance to the school in 1905, elevates Chaplin's status in the eyes of your family to the point where if you were still painting icons, they would demand you paint him.

What did he see in the drawings, in you? Was it a talent that demanded to be fed, or were you simply a vehicle, the chance for a "small deed," that most Russian of intentions, the expression of a progressive's desire to better society? Are you the particular reason or the general? Was he a man simply waiting for the right time and circumstance to fulfill these impulses, all his motives finding voice in a young boy drawing pictures in his office?

The general or the particular. You hope it was the particular. It mattered to you that you were worthy of his efforts.

You remember watching the man as he reviewed plans for a heating system to be installed in a factory, how his eyes took in details and made sense of them in a way that was impossible for others. You recall his voice, that tone that you have come to identify with competence—never raised, a quality that extended to the household into which you were invited. At the end of the summer you shared with his children, you thanked the younger daughter for her kindness, and she looked at you quizzically. You could only explain that your clothes embarrassed you and you thanked her for not mocking them.

"Papa forbids it," she said.

Debut: Paris, June 21st, 1925

The flash welds your eyes shut and a second sun throbs, trailing off to deep space. The sulphur smell drifts over you next, along with the wreaths of smoke, and finally you can see again.

"Un autre, Monsieur Melnikov, s'il vous plait," the photographer says, and you nod your assent. He lifts his tripod and camera with such tenderness, backing up, his footsteps soundless. You can see what will come next, a shot up the stairway, with you standing along the sheer wall of the pavilion. He wants scale. (Another photographer, with whom you argued, as if understanding his intent, took a picture of you from below as you stood cross-armed in front of the pavilion, making it seem as though you dwarfed the building, as though you were about to abandon the desire to build and instead head toward Paris to devour those buildings that did not bear your name.)

You turn your head to the left. All of Paris is talking about you. Hoffman has written approvingly about you in the papers. Le Corbusier has shaken your hand and pronounced you a visionary. The pavilion has been described as a revolutionary building, like nothing seen before, a model of the Constructivist aesthetic. But they don't really know the building. They don't know you.

The Pavilion's admirers walk through the main hall and tell you they have never seen anything like it. But none of them has ever seen your preliminary sketches for the Lenin sarcophagus—your preferred design rejected in favor of a simplified glass case that embarrassed you for the way it made the leader look like baked goods on display. If they had agreed to your choice of sarcophagus, perhaps the Parisians would have seen this pavilion not as a revolution but as the next necessary step. They would have found the pavilion's floor plan already set, noticed how the precisely measured angles of the glass vault that was never built for the great leader were reborn in the pavilion. You explain nothing. It is enough for you to know that you have built what they would not let you build before. If anyone had known you, perhaps they would have expected to see how you defied space and admitted light. They would have known that the Soviet Union's official pavilion for the Paris Exposition was not revolutionary, but simply a statement that any architect wishes to make, that the sentiments that devised such design will exist, must exist outside of revolutions, and will certainly outlast them.

He motions for you to move to your right. *"Monsieur, pourriez-vous soulever votre main et toucher le mur?"*

"Certainment."

Straighten your tie. There is talk that Le Corbusier has secured a commission for you, a parking garage in Paris. Rodchenko, who is miserable here and revels in his misery, has told you to be wary of him, of his flattery and promises.

But you can already see the design, the flow of vehicles through the structure like corpuscles through a body. Order from chaos. Order never imposed, but always derived.

It was standing here with Anna only a few days earlier that you asked her if she would be happy in Paris. There is work here, you wanted to say, but what you meant was there was possibility here. It was a question you were asking yourself, of course, trying to find some design of your true feelings in her response. She was taken aback at the thought of not going home. "Paris is beautiful" was all she said, and you were unsure if this was her argument for staying or something said to obscure the argument.

Between the photographer's requests for positioning as he adjusts his aim for the shot, he is solemn. The man is dressed formally and works in silence under the black hood that tents up around the back of his apparatus. A black-sleeved arm protrudes from the hood, jutting into the air and wavering there, supporting the little platform on which sits the incendiary powder for the flash.

A ridiculous-looking animal. An emu in mourning clothes. A photographer. You grin at the thought, and the photographer emerges from the depths of this strange animal as if to chastise you. He has an aesthetic order to maintain as well. At the last second, just before the flash, you pull your hand away from the wall. You wonder about this later, once you see that particular photo that shows your hand caught in midair, mid-movement. Did you intend to move your hand? The photographer will be displeased by this image—the seeming intrusion of a blurred bird in flight—but you are captivated by the impression that the photo gives, particularly that one cannot tell if your hand is moving toward or away from the building. One more secret kept to yourself.

But at the moment, all you feel is another explosion of light. These Parisian cloudbursts. Their echoes already approaching. You steady yourself.

"Merci, monsieur."

GOLDEN SEASON

You don't sleep. You tell yourself it is because the noise is ceaseless. The humming of some continuous cycle. A machine dream that inspires fear until you realize that it is the dream you have created, your experience. Awaken, and the noise continues. A new Moscow is rising.

The projects arrive, one after another, a proposal for the Kauchuk Factory Club on the very day when you open the Leyland garage. The Burevestnik Club arrives on its heels. A parade of commissions. You are too busy to acknowledge the way it makes you feel. It seems natural that your vision should be embraced, that others feel the same way, because you build for them, for the vision that you all share. You don't see Anna for days, and when you do, the thing you notice first about her is that she has another letter that has arrived for you, in it a proposal for a building.

In the midst of this season of work, there is word that you have been chosen to redesign the Arbat. Nothing makes you happier than this thought, that the grand market itself would be trusted to you. The truth is that you want to refuse, to tell them that a market can only ever design itself, that you can observe and facilitate, but you can only ever assist the design. But there are always improvements to be made. You imagine the flow of people, less chaotic now, market day graced by this movement, graced by the beauty of simple ideas. But this is only rumor, distant.

Around you, Moscow is being rebuilt. And unlike Petersburg—built on a royal whim, willed into existence on the edge of a bog, with avenues lined by the imitations of other cultures—Moscow has always been here, half European, half Asian, the very core of Russia itself. Moscow listens to no czar, but changes like a huge organism, changes according to the needs and the dreams and the will of its citizens. You feel this. You will be a part of this. The Svoboda Factory Club is next, and the Rusakov Workers' Club follows, each building the necessary precursor to what follows. When Rusakov is opened, you stand with Anna on Stromynka Street, in the cantilever shadows and are asked what effect you were striving for. You find the question perplexing. There is no effect here, you want to tell them, looking up, and for a moment you understand that you cannot control the effect your work has on others. After a certain point, it is not yours. As sad as this is, it allows you a particular freedom. You are able to look at the building with fresh eyes, the eyes of a peasant wandering in from the countryside, the eyes of a bird in flight. You tell them it is nothing more, nothing less, than a tensed muscle. And with this they are satisfied.

Krivoarbatsky Lane/Anna's Home

She walks around the building and smiles, treading carefully and contemplating each step in the muddy ground of the work site. She is concerned about her shoes: red leather, bought in Paris and still prized by her. Polished and tended to, they are still new-looking, two years after their purchase. You told her only that you wanted to meet, that you had a surprise for her, and so she had no idea that she would be tramping around in the mud. The pride that you felt, the need to share what you have built, has dissipated.

It makes you wish that you had delayed this moment at least until the facade had been finished. Never show a building that has not been completed. How could you have forgotten this? The masonry work that had so impressed you, draws only puzzlement from her. Is this what I am supposed to live in? You feel she must think you have lost your mind. The brickwork and curved walls are quite clearly absurd; the future home that you have wished to show must look to her like the base of a huge smokestack. It would be impossible for her to see a home in this. You imagined that she would see it as you did, from the point of its conception, that she would see your life together. She smiles again, and this smile, its condescension, its benevolent regret, causes such pain in you, more acute than any pang at being passed over in a competition.

"Where is the door supposed to be?" she asks. She hates it.

"The other side," you reply. "The door will face south, of course, toward the street."

She walks around the base of the building and you follow, your attention trailing from the heels of her shoes to the footprints she leaves in the clay. At some point, you stop and then turn and begin walking in the opposite direction, chastising yourself for allowing an opinion, even Anna's, to cause you to question yourself. This is the building, the only building it could be. It will be beautiful, you think. You have seen it for years.

She will see it, too. You chide yourself that it is as much

a lack of confidence in her, in her trust in your vision, as it is in your own work. You owe her more than this. By this time, she has walked completely around the building and now approaches you. You are face-to-face. This is weakness. Years from this moment, you will try to remember what she is saying now or the way in which she says it, but all is overshadowed by the surprising expression on her face, the very details that bespeak pleasure, the designs of happiness.

St. Nikolai the Carpenter

One amendment to the design. As the masons are working, you realize that the dome of St. Nikolai the Carpenter is visible from the entrance of your house. Until this moment, the windows have functioned as portals, admitting light to the house. But the site of the dome causes you to sit down with your plans, calling over Gusev. You explain yourself and he mulls over the possibilities. "But Mikhail Vasilevich," you say, "there is only one possibility," and he takes off his cap and that expression appears—wry smile or grimace; you're never exactly sure which. He will speak to the masons, he says, and walks away.

A west-facing window through which the dome can be seen. The height of the window is such that the church is visible only when the occupant bends or kneels. It is the one aspect of the building that pleases you most, your work a lens through which one small part of the world is understood, through which the occupant must be engaged, must seek an expression of his own character in order to find a moment of particular beauty.

You consider it for a long time before deciding to make this window different from the others. Gusev objects, citing unity of design and that a break from hexagons would be tantamount to defacement. But this window is different; it comes from another impulse, and that impulse must be acknowledged. The upper and lower corners of a hexagon are nullified and its shape becomes an irregular octagon, with St. Nikolai appropriately framed.

You bend every day. You receive your reward. You understand the impulse. St. Nikolai is destroyed three years later—some larger plan that you are not a party to, perhaps nothing more than Stalin's whim—but you still stoop, the action now sanctifying a small and anonymous patch of gray sky over Moscow.

YOU ARE A FORMALIST

You receive a message. There is a warning. And then a meeting.

You are a formalist.

Where does a judgment like this come from? Does it originate in the air, or in the minds of men? Perhaps it is in the buildings themselves, a flaw (not a flaw—a feature) designed to provoke this reaction, which, in turn, challenges the architect to defend.

The judgment has been years in the making. You remember the morning of February 18, 1936, a copy of *Komsomolskaia Pravda* left at your door, the page folded back that contained the anonymous letter accusing you of ignoring the precepts of socialist realism. A fortnight before, Shostakovich had been publically branded a formalist for his Lady Macbeth of Mtsensk, and now it was your turn. What injured you more were the attacks in the *Architectural Gazette* a week later, one by your old friend Shchusev, already decrying your obstinacy in failing to mend your ways.

Whatever the origin of this judgment, it sets down in a specific place, like any species of carrion bird; in this case, it is the first-ever Congress of the Union of Soviet Architects. You are invited to address the congress. You are informed that you have the opportunity to explain yourself. You are told, parenthetically, that the congress promises to be a gala event. An American, Mr. Frank Lloyd Wright, will be in attendance as an honored guest of the congress. You assume Mr. Wright is not a formalist.

The first thing a person facing such an accusation would do is find out who was responsible for the charge, but you needn't ask. You know your accusers. Chief among them is Karo Alabian, who, as president of the Union of Soviet Architects, will deliver the keynote address to the congress. It was Alabian, given strength by your dismissal from the Architectural Institute, who began his attacks on you in the journal of the Union of Soviet Architects the year before. You remembered reading Anna the concluding paragraph at the time, chuckling as if it were a valedictory:

"He wants only to be exceptionally bold and unusual—he seeks to be original for its own sake. In short, Melnikov's fundamental and sole aim is to produce an architecture that no one else has ever created."

Wasn't he your student at the Vkhutemas? Anna asks and you nod. You don't tell her about the disagreements you've had with the man, how, despite the success of the Paris Exposition and the renown you've brought to Russian architecture, Alabian removed any mention of your name alone from the student publications he edited at the Vkhutemas. You don't tell Anna that he has built only one building, the Central Theatre of the Russian Army, which, in an instance of uncanny aesthetic concordance, perfectly reflected its maker's character through its grandiose vulgarity.

This time, you decide to defend yourself. Let the people of Moscow decide which architect speaks with their voice. If they decide against me, against my work, you think, then let them begin the demolition. I will be the first to swing the hammer. This will be a moment for all of Moscow, all the Soviet Union to hear the principles on which their builders create. You will appear before the congress, you decide. Let us talk architecture, then. You hearten yourself with talk like this, of the nonsense of the charge. What is a formalist? These meaningless words and their libelous intent will be cast back onto those who uttered them; they will be exposed for their jealousies and vanities. Have they forgotten the Paris Exposition and prestige it brought to the entire country? Have they forgotten who founded the Vkhutemas? You have your allies, and you automatically begin reciting their names, an act that causes you to feel an inaugural moment of panic, but the names arrive easily. Names of students, colleagues, names of others whom you've helped. You can strike Shchushev's name from the list. So be it. Better to know your enemies.

This will be a moment when all of Moscow will be forced to acknowledge the work you have done and how this casts into sharp relief the meagerness of your accusers.

But at night, darker thoughts arrive. Anna, who has listened approvingly as you nursed and fed your rebuttal, lies silently beside you, and her reassurances sleep with her. You feel the creeping threat. The condemnation is arbitrary. And while you thought this was a meaningless charge, its meaninglessness is its very strength. In a way, the judgment has already been rendered. In two years of otherwise-intense construction activity in Moscow, you have had no work. Your entries do not advance at competitions.

It is a simple equation. To work, to receive commissions, one must adhere to the tenets of socialist realism. Formalism is incompatible with socialist realism. You are a formalist. This is not a difference of tastes that can be debated. The congress will declare a failure on your part for being obstinate, as well as incriminating your colleagues for failing to "educate" you. You understand them. They will make you disown your work. To rehabilitate, you will have to say everything has been a mistake, that every impulse that guided you was in error.

Explain yourself.

You can hear the room breathe. Across the city, snow falls and your buildings sigh and begin to disappear. You have been explaining yourself all your life, with everything you have built. You have spent twenty years struggling to build a case against yourself.

You are a formalist.

March 5, 1953

It is complicated. Grief always is. Since the announcement of Stalin's death, the radio plays a continuous tribute to him, with occasional breaks for music that he admired. The city is motionless and you cannot tell if it is exhausted or recoiling. Either way, there is silence.

Anna, as usual, shows her emotions honestly. You warn her to temper her glee, but she holds him responsible for your exile. The next may be different, Anna says. There is always the opportunity for rehabilitation. The next man may value your work; perhaps he will be a man of culture who may understand that the architectural reputation of the USSR has suffered and that you are one who can redeem it.

You nod in agreement, wordless in the face of devotion so unwavering. It would be inappropriate to tell her that you think the next man will be the same as the last. A touch less brutal. Perhaps more. The impulse will be the same. It is simply another constraint that an architect must contend with. The realities of a difficult site. She would understand, but it is just as important to you that she doesn't need to.

She circles the drawing table before leaving, not noticing that you are already drawing preliminary sketches for a memorial, visible from all corners of Moscow.

April 3, 1973, Krivoarbatsky Lane, Moscow

The two men, a professor of architecture and his student, sit across from you. Between sips of tea, their gaze climbs up the wall and nestles at a spot just under the ceiling. They are the latest pilgrims to present themselves at your house. For a chat. An audience. They wish to see the house. But what these men really want to know, like all the others who came before, is how you managed to survive without building anything for forty years. Do you see the incomprehension in the eyes of the student? These are my eyes, taking in the details of the drawings you show us, the plans you knew would never be realized. These are my eyes, watching you answer that, to the contrary, you have been busy these forty years, reconstructing the Arbat and rebuilding Moscow. Grand avenues and pavilions. An entire city in darkness. I want to ask you how you lived like this. I will need to know what sort of desire can give such sustenance and yet does not devour a man. Tell me.

But there is no answer.

There is no answer because there has been no principled stance, only you, squirming away in your monument. Your crypt. But the boy in front of you does not know this yet, does not know the difference between dissent and condescension. Between courage and mythmaking. But he will learn. Your only explanation is to show us more drawings, four decades spread out on parchment beneath your hands. You have built nothing.

You have been afraid. You have been a fool; you have been a man living on a promise that was never realized, hiding in your work. You smile, you crazy, scared old man. But you have built nothing.

At the bottom of the last page, he sees, in the familiar loops of his own handwriting, dated the day of his accident, a final annotation: "I could never go on like this. I cannot go on. I am so sorry. Martin."

Chapter 18

It was only after Martin found himself outside—breathing hard and feeling his heart pound its deep, visceral protest up and into his throat—that he understood he had fled his own house. The house was to have been his sanctuary: He had come here thinking he would find comfort, the traces and reassurances of a previous life, from which he could make sense of the world and perhaps even build again. The house would be a source, an answer. The house would tell him the truth. And, in a perverse way, the house had obliged, telling him everything he needed to know about himself, a judgment harsh enough to leave him trembling in exile on the back patio. He stood in its shadow and felt the measure of darkness it cast.

He turned away from the house and walked down the gentle incline toward the water's edge, understanding fully what he had escaped from, trying to avoid thinking of what he'd just read, not because it perplexed him but because it made perfect sense. He had given up. There had been no heroic fight, no grand plan to wrest the consulate project away from his former firm. There had been only surrender: outlasted by clients and partners, paid off to go away, dealt with. The only plan he'd come up with was an ending, and now that he'd found an artifact of his own hopelessness, the crash was not a mere incident clouded in amnesia, but an event he could construct, richer and sadder and more cinematic than any simple recollection of events. Melnikov had been in his mind when he awoke because he'd been there on that last night: the all-purpose foil, the patron saint of failed architects ushering him into a crypt to await commissions and acclaim that would never come. This would be his memory now, the provenance of *him,* and the thought of this brought him to the edge of the dock.

The cool grip of lake water on his right hand, the bottom indistinct in silt and moss-coated rocks. The other hand dove in, automatically following, coming alive as it hit the water. His body took shape here; the world that eluded him returned, he thought as he slouched forward, kicking away the last of the reeds that rimmed the lake. The momentary sting of water against his knees and thighs, grazing his chin and causing him to close his mouth. It would be silent underwater. Quiet and full. Twenty strokes would take him to a part of the lake where the bottom under his feet would be lost, where a man in his condition could easily falter.

He imagined both hands trailing, birthing a series of wakes, twin trails of him fanning out, canceling out or doubling him. He turned to his right, uncertain of the impulse itself, uncertain why he should wade in that direction. When he came to the small dock—its shadow and mass rising silently from the water, surprising him—he lifted his right hand and steadied himself as he began to float.

Martin dipped his face into the cold lake water, his whole body trembling for a moment until the water was no longer cold, no longer water, until the surface of his body disappeared in the water. With his right arm tethering him to the dock, he floated, left side down, immersed in space and darkness, listening to the slow cycling of his breathing, imagining there was a heart to him, its rhythms inaudible even in the silence of the lake.

The cold water gave a small scorpion sting to the inside of his left ear, but it was not enough to rouse him to move. He floated and tried to clear his mind.

And then it began, with what could only be described as the sensation of *something touching him,* but it was more than that; it was the curious moment of information intersecting, of sensation and space and time aligning to tell him that something was touching his left foot. He reflexively kicked his legs and then, without being completely aware, he felt his left hand brushing along the outer aspect of his calf, exploring the sensation, confirming nothing was there, and then the hand dug in its nails for good measure, and he did not feel pain as much as certainty that this was his hand and this was his leg and that he was aware of them in a way that he hadn't been before.

He opened his eyes and looked up to the edge of the dock, which was spinning uncontrollably, the early-morning sky capsizing into the water over and over again in such a way that his only response was to clamp his hand onto the dock more tightly. He would have simply closed his eyes and held on, but he felt an urgent and inexplicable need to keep his eyes open.

The dock had changed. Even as it somersaulted over him—and this was, to Martin, the most amazing thing, that its spinning seemed altogether unremarkable—the dock was clearly different, and not in a way that was immediately discernible. He watched the structure for a few moments, trying to understand just what was so unusual about it now. It seemed to Martin that his vision had changed: The dock was revealed, longer than he had noted a minute before, stretching off into the west, where it sank into the lake. In the distance, several small white triangles had materialized, clustered together at the western edge of the lake, where the wind was good. But at the same time he was able to see more, he became aware that a crescent-shaped shade had been cast across his vision on the left, and he reflexively covered and uncovered his left eye, thinking that something was blocking his vision. Part of the left upper quadrant was blank. Gone. How had he not known? He could see more, but he could see less. He couldn't understand if this meant he was getting better or worse.

He log-rolled in the water and twisted his head fully to the left, a movement that felt at first indefinite and then, as he understood what he was looking at, had an ache of certainty. It was clear to him. His left leg and arm materialized beside him, as though the anesthesia that hid them had just worn off. The limbs seemed to announce their presence, gaining heft and volume. Aching. And with this, it seemed to Martin that what he had experienced of his body before, the sense that closing his eyes would return him to normal, seemed ludicrous and naïve, that along with their miraculous appearance, his left leg and arm were also correcting him, chastising him for his presumptuousness. He panicked, thinking he should get to a doctor, that this was a real emergency. He thought about calling out to someone, but he realized he wouldn't know what to say.

He stopped moving, stopped struggling, and let himself float on his left side, his right arm still tethering him to the dock. The water around him settled. The world's spinning slowed enough that when he looked down into the water's reflection, he saw himself emerge and was shocked to find a mouth that gaped open and hung grimly unbalanced, as though unable to ask the necessary questions about what had happened to him. He closed his eyes, but this gave him no respite from the sense that something was wrong as he became fully aware of his body in a way that he had not experienced before, suddenly aware of it as profoundly imperfect, a left side that seemed to hang dumbly and responded with only grudging acknowledgment. He felt himself breathing deeply, his mouth and nose hissing away, barely above the water-line.

Martin rolled onto his back and concentrated instead on the pale blue wash of early morning sky. He found comfort in this. The sky did not surprise him, and he imagined being able to concentrate on one small region, one acre of sky, that would sit above him and be his reference point.

His breathing slowed and he felt as though he could drift into sleep, away from thoughts of his body as anything but normal. It had been a hallucination, he told himself, a dream perhaps, but at any rate something *unreal,* and any thought of what he had experienced was then not forgotten as much as abandoned for something else more convincing. But he could not lose the sense that something had happened to him, a visceral tug receding ever deeper, echoing away. What remained was a dawning sense of dread. He stood up in the water beside the dock, the dock solid under his right hand. Beside his hand was a foot, which he followed up, to find his brother standing there, looking down at him.

"You okay?"

"Never better. Could you help me out, please?"

"Here, grab my hand," Brendan said, and crouched, grasping Martin's hand and then leaning back to hoist him out of the water. Martin hooked a leg up on the dock but could not get to his feet. He rolled onto the platform, breathing heavily as Brendan sat down beside him.

"What were you doing in there?"

"Nothing."

"You were in the lake, Martin. What were you doing?"

"That's not important," Martin said, and heard his brother's sighing noise.

"Brendan."

"Yes?"

"I need you to be honest with me."

"Yeah, sure."

Martin looked over at Brendan, tried to find his brother's face, searching for a feature that he could latch onto. But he was lost again, adrift in space whose strangeness was inseparable from its familiarity. He reached out for his brother, his hand falling on Brendan's left shoulder.

"Tell me what you know about the night I was in the accident."

"I only know what the police told me, Martin."

"I want you to be honest with me."

"Sure."

"Did you know I was trying to kill myself?"

Chapter 19

Brendan sat on the dock beside Martin and told him what he knew about the crash, the details from the police, the thirty-foot length of garden hose and spool of duct tape, receipts of the newly purchased objects still in the bag. He let the inferences settle in the silence that followed and prepared himself for whatever reaction his brother might have. Martin said nothing.

Brendan led Martin back to the house and into the living room. He peeled Martin's wet pajamas off and helped him stop shivering by rubbing him with a towel. He then eased him onto the couch, watching with some amazement as Martin fell asleep with the fluid rapidity of a small child. Brendan went back to his room and searched through his agenda for the name of the doctor Martin was to see the following week. He called the clinic, only to be told that the doctor was still on vacation and if there was a problem that couldn't wait, he should take his brother to an emergency room. He had thoughts of calling Feingold or Martin's daughters, both thoughts so lacking in promise that neither prompted him even to search his phone for their numbers. Uncertain of what he should do, he returned to the living room, where he sat and watched Martin. His brother did not stir.

Brendan had entered Martin's room and found the model destroyed, pulverized pieces scattered over the desk and the floor around it. On the nearby bed lay a number of sheets of paper, turned over, as though they'd just been read, and a single sheet, the last one upturned. Brendan shouted for Martin but heard no reply and immediately went to the window. The view from Martin's room was similar to his, the back patio and the shoreline, with the lake beyond. It was from this vantage point that Brendan caught a glimpse of Martin rooting through the long grass that bordered the water. As Martin waded into the lake, Brendan stood in his brother's room, edging closer to the window to witness what would happen next. Martin stumbled as he moved deeper into water, and at that moment Brendan recalled the roadside restaurant they had stopped at on their way up to the lake, how Martin had eluded him and gone off wandering, and how he had chased him down just short of the highway. At the time, it seemed to him as though he had pursued his brother without delay, but remembering it from the second floor of the country house, he was suddenly aware of having stood outside the restaurant, coffee cups in hand, watching his brother stagger toward potential doom. He had watched. He had done nothing. He was not certain how long he'd paused, but the intensity of the shame he felt seemed to time it perfectly. It was this shame that propelled him as he pounded down the stairs and raced though the main room toward the sliding door that led to the outside, an eye on the water, an eye on the dock, wanting to do nothing but retrieve his brother.

And even now, he watched his brother in that way that he recognized was both clinical and brotherly. The scientist, the sentinel. An appeal to both sides of the argument for his being at his brother's side throughout all this. From a chair across the room, Brendan studied his brother's breathing. Seemingly untroubled by the conclusions he'd come to, Martin turned and opened his eyes briefly, enough for Brendan to wonder what his brother saw, what he could possibly see. Brendan had told Martin that he had no idea whether he had wanted to end his life that night in February, and this calmed his brother so dramatically that it seemed to be all the rationale he needed to create the lie.

He wondered what Martin experienced on that highway in February as he pulled his car to a halt. If he saw snow falling through the headlights of traffic in the oncoming lane or just the soft blue-and-orange background buzz of the car's instrument panel. He wondered if he played with the dials of the radio, looking for music that would ease him into closing his eyes or convince him otherwise. The despair of last acts. *This is where we come to a stop.*

God, we are the same, he wanted to say to his brother. *We're the same.* There must exist, Brendan thought, a particular gene for destruction for them to have lived entirely different lives and yet come to the same conclusion. A gene was a good explanation. As good as sadness or anomie or a lack of God or a serotonin problem.

Martin muttered in his sleep. The last things he saw, Brendan thought, did they comfort him? What had he seen?

Brendan, for his part, remembered that he had seen only red. If he had been asked to describe the color (and no one had asked, not his partners or the Veterinary Disciplinary Board, which reviewed any case where significant amounts of ketamine had gone missing), he would have had to describe it as a buoyant red. Balloon red. Just as well he'd never had to describe it.

What he could never tell people is that the color was only a herald of the calm that the drug invariably brought, that it was a marker of respite and made the hours pass like minutes, shrinking time in a way that reassured him like nothing else could in the months after Rita's death.

And then he remembered awakening. Animals sometimes

snapped when they awoke from ketamine, and he always thought that it was the drug itself, the flushing of some synapse that caused them to strike out blindly at something nearby, the triggering of a reflex. But when he awoke, he'd felt none of that. No need to do anything except listen to himself breathe. To feel the air entering his lungs and warming before cycling out again, and Rita somehow wasn't gone forever, but simply *beyond this.* The peace that that brought was beyond description. Beyond redness or the obliteration of time or anything else that he experienced when he slipped the catheter under the skin and started running the solution.

And then came a time when the sting of the catheter was almost as potent as the first swell of the high (thank you, Dr. Pavlov), and then it took only the thin but authoritative embrace of the tourniquet and finally simply opening the door to his office with a bottle in his hand to be sufficient for him to see the first pixels of red, to imagine the color arriving, blossoming as he sat alone in his office. Rita disappeared amid all this, of course. Rita was forgotten first in the red, and then she disappeared in the work it took to procure the ketamine on a regular basis, to fabricate the reasons for needing it and the explanations for suddenly having to go back to his office. But he had been the boss. No one contested his prerogative.

He wondered whether Martin had felt the same thing on the roadside as he had that last time he sat in a recliner and prepared himself for a final taste of red and relief, whether sadness was just the narrowing of all possibilities into an inevitable last act, an act that paradoxically seemed to offer hope only because all other acts had lost that capacity. Once that calculation happened, it was impossible to escape the logic that followed. He had tired of waking up. The solution was, therefore, not to wake up anymore.

He opened his eyes in a hospital ICU with a respiratory technologist in greens adjusting the parameters of a ventilator. Later that day, a staff doctor explained what had happened: an infusion error probably, something that would have led to his death had not ketamine been such a damn fine anesthetic agent, with properties that prevented his blood pressure from dropping, carrying him through that long night of colors and the darkness that followed. That had been his only error, a miscalculation that allowed him to survive that last infusion and made it necessary to answer for his actions. The first inquisitor was the psychiatrist who appeared with dismal regularity at his bedside. It seemed easier, and preferable, as he didn't wish to have anyone's sympathy, to convince the psychiatrist that he was a reckless junkie rather than a hapless depressive, and so he disavowed any suicidal intent. The psychiatrist nodded and left, another truth revealed.

He thought, once, in the first few days in the intensive care unit, that he had caught a glimpse of one of his sons, David or Paul, standing at the foot of his bed. It was a purely visual memory, suitably fleeting amid the chuffs and beepings of ventilators and monitors. He was never sure if it was real, and in their brief discussions afterward, it was never discussed.

There were other repercussions, of course. His former partners, now answering to a corporate head office, had no hesitation in surveying the in-house pharmacy records and thus discovered the pattern that one would expect. After that, it was just the formality of a series of letters informing him of his immediate suspension—not even the visit, he could have told Martin, not even the fruit basket—and going on to say that the matter was being referred to disciplinary committee of their professional association. The only hint of leniency would come with the sentence telling him that "no formal criminal complaint will be pursued." He was spared having to explain himself at the hearing. A disciplinary panel is no place for a discussion of red or loneliness.

It was early afternoon when, Martin began to stir. Brendan said nothing as Martin sat up and looked around the room, nothing as his brother's right hand reached up and touched his left temple, running the fingertips across his forehead to the ridge above his right eye. He wanted to ask Martin what he saw. If he saw anything. *Did you see red?*

"I should take you back to Montreal."

"I don't want to go," Martin said, groaning as he adjusted his position on the couch. "You think I was out there to end it."

"I know what they found in your car. Maybe you decided against it. But I do know that finding you in the lake in your pajamas is a bit worrisome."

"I didn't plan that."

"That's reassuring."

"The house isn't having a great effect on me."

"Then let's get out of here. Let's head back to Montreal. Besides, you have doctors appointments."

"That's not until next week."

"We can head back tonight. Rest up."

"I can't go back right now," said Martin. "I'm not ready for that. I want to go to Detroit."

Part III

And even I, who would like to keep the two cities distinct in my memory, can speak only of the one, because the recollection of the other, in the lack of words to fix it, has been lost.

—Italo Calvino, *Invisible Cities*

Chapter 20

Brendan always chose the bridge over the tunnel, and he would think of nothing of traveling the extra distance, as he had done this time, in order to take the Ambassador into Detroit. The waits at Customs were similar, and he was not given to claustrophobia to explain his decision. Maybe it was still the soldier in him, needing to see for himself the territory he would have to negotiate rather than emerging from darkness already behind the lines.

The traffic slowed to a stop on the downslope of the bridge and he looked over the city. To the east, he recognized the twin spires of Ste. Anne de Detroit, and looming behind that was the massive rectangular form of the Michigan Central Station. It had not been far from here, one Tuesday morning ten years before, during a visit to his mother, that he happened to be at the correct spot to catch a glimpse of the sun shining through the windows of that abandoned building. He remembered how the building had been transformed from a silhouette to something suddenly illuminated by hundreds of points of light. It had looked to him as though the insides of the building had begun to glow. And then, as the car advanced, he became aware that it was simply sunlight passing through nothingness, through an empty shell. Still, he had found it beautiful, and whenever he had tried to explain why—the contingencies of time of day and the absolutely perfect angle, the transience of the whole thing and just the fact that he had turned his head to the right at precisely the correct moment for some unknown reason—he was always lost for words.

As he continued down the bridge, the distance he had traveled caused the Central Station to appear to be directly behind the church, its upper floors framed between the spires, in his sights. Farther to the east, the city, in the last moments of a flattering twilight, looked monumental, sentinels of abandonment that could still pass for a skyline. He had awakened Martin, and his brother gamely stared out the window for a moment as Brendan pointed to landmarks they'd both known from their childhoods. But beyond this gesture, there was no interest. The Renaissance Center gave way to the remaining Gothic towers of a jagged downtown. They were home.

Brendan understood that even if he had wanted to describe Detroit to people back in New York, he could not. It was not for lack of words but because he detested the way the words sounded as they left his mouth. He silently despised the way the name of the city had been revised from De-TROIT to DEE-troit but held his tongue because he knew how this change came about, that it was not through an edict imposed. It was just the name of the city now, ask any of its citizens; if it were some form of tyranny that renamed his hometown, it was the tyranny of demographics, and this thought, and his response to it, made him sink.

He reassured himself he was not racist—he was a fair man, with black friends and trusted colleagues, and he had employed a vast army, all of whom he valued for their individual competences—and he reviewed the evidence often enough to understand what these perpetual reassurances must mean, what insecurities they addressed. He wanted to tell someone how it grieved him to think this way, that he tried to think every way except this way (and there was ample alternative evidence to invoke when the decline of Detroit was discussed: the failure of the Big Three, globalization, the city's abandonment by people like him, the almost-expected—but still surpassing—venalities of the mayor's office balanced by the purer village idiocy of the lame duck in the White House). He wanted to hate it all without race invoked, to tell himself that his anger was valid and not the easily dismissed rantings of some cracker. But DEE-troit was always there to goad him with its gleeful squalor. DEE-troit with its systemic arson. DEE-troit with its buildings emptying still.

Martin had been noticeably docile for the entire trip down, quiet enough that Brendan had almost convinced himself of a nostalgia for the flare-ups of bellicose paranoia that had gone on before. Martin's behavior, almost since his awakening at the Dunes, had been difficult, but in a straightforward way—in a way that a snarling dog is always preferable, in its clarity of threat, to the quiet dog that is about to snap. Silence was simply more difficult to assess, and looking across at him, he was unsure if Martin was dazed or ruminating, exhausted or spiraling toward blacker thoughts. During one of their rest stops, with Martin safely confined by a bathroom stall, he had stepped out and made another call to the psychiatrist whom Martin was scheduled to see, but again he got the voice mail.

And so, with his brother mute to conversation and indifferent to diversion, Brendan turned on the radio and scanned stations, cycling through the available choices and settling on a neutral-sounding NPR station, relatively lacto-ovo compared to the anarcho-vegan NPR outlet that he regularly sampled and turned off at home in New York.

Fifty-five floors above the Detroit River, the outskirts of Windsor fading into the more distant darkness of southern Ontario,

Brendan sat up in bed and arranged the pillows behind him. Martin had awakened long enough to stand beside him at the Marriott's reception desk before wordlessly slipping under the covers of the other bed, where he now emitted an intermittent rasp, an exact impersonation of a screen door closing. The flash of changing channels in the darkened room was not enough to rouse him.

"You awake?" Brendan asked.

He turned up the television, not enough to disturb his brother, but loud enough that he would be distracted from reading the news ticker that ran along the bottom of the screen. The scrolling messages always managed to agitate him, with their endless haikus of vague information that drew his eyes to the last words when the rest of the message had already disappeared . . . toward the earth (What? Life-giving sunshine? An asteroid?) . . . vitamin can kill (Too much? Too little? Which vitamin? WHICH VITAMIN?). Television news had reduced him to Charlie Chaplin in *Modern Times,* the hapless victim of too much velocity, frozen by the truths streaming by him while he was undoubtedly busy poisoning himself with the wrong vitamins while waiting for the asteroid to strike. Like most nights, he would find the three main news channels and bounce from one to the next, hoping to triangulate something resembling the truth.

Chapter 21

Martin allowed himself to be led down by Brendan to the hotel's restaurant for breakfast, holding on to his brother's arm more tightly than Brendan was used to. Brendan studied him at the table as they ate, his brother intently spearing pieces of fruit, working the right side of the plate while melon balls and a small stem of grapes accumulated on the other side, untouched, unnoticed.

As Martin searched for his coffee cup, Brendan reached over and rotated the plate. When Martin returned his attention to the plate, he simply resumed eating; never questioning where the new supply of fruit had appeared from.

"I don't have anything for her," Martin said.

"I'm sorry?"

"A present. I don't have a present."

"It's okay; she doesn't want a present."

"Still."

"She might not remember it's her birthday."

"Then why are we visiting today?"

"Well, because *we* remembered it's her birthday. We can pick up something."

"There's a florist on the way," Martin said, and paused. He had eaten the last grape and now studied the stem, which looked like a felled maple in winter. He looked up from the plate. "When did you know about it?"

"About what, Martin?"

"That I tried to kill myself."

"It doesn't help to talk about this."

"I think you knew. Maybe from the moment you heard about my accident. Maybe before they told you."

"How would I know something like that about you? I didn't know *you.*"

"Why are you here?"

"I'm family."

Martin leaned closer. "Why are you here? Is it just to confirm what you always thought about me?"

"Calm down, Martin."

"I think you like the thought of its being a riddle."

Brendan slowly rotated his head from side to side. "It's not a riddle, Martin; it's your life. Do you remember what you felt that night? Your intent?"

"No."

"Do you want to kill yourself now?"

"No."

"Then you probably decided against it back then."

"Well now, I suppose that's as life-affirming as this will get."

"You sound like Feingold."

"Maybe Feingold wasn't so bad."

"I never said she was bad."

Martin stared at him and Brendan smiled the sort of smile that felt to him like the mask that hotel clerks and flight attendants wore, the type of expression that politely severed further communication. Period. He wondered whether this was decipherable to his brother, who continued to stare at him in a way that told him that it was not. The grapes were gone from Martin's plate now, leaving behind a stem that looked like a miniature maple felled in midwinter.

They ate breakfast together and said nothing more. It was as if they were kids again, heads down over bowls of cereal as their mother moved around them, between them. The silence made Brendan think how odd it was that he couldn't remember a word that they'd ever said to each other, while he had more vivid memories for the nonverbal things: the feel of flannel pajamas, the sound of his little brother repeatedly kicking his chair. Him kicking back. Words were nothing. Words were sounds that they used to hide themselves in.

"Tell me about your wife," Martin said.

"I'd rather not."

"Okay."

"I'm sorry. I spent some time in therapy after she died and I think . . . I think I did the work then, you know. . . ."

Martin nodded and smiled. Not the dogged acknowledging nod of someone fresh from the rehab wards of the Dunes, but something more nuanced, respectfully letting Brendan out of the conversation. He nodded again, very understandingly. Brendan studied his brother, now a Buddha of compassion. He tried to smile in appreciation at Martin's gesture, so rich in sophisticated emotion that it was demanding to be replayed in Brendan's head as it was simultaneously occurring. Iterations of Martin smiling. Parallel smiles, not just of commiseration but also empathy, yes, and solidarity, too. He recognized that this was the sort of gesture that should have strengthened whatever bond they had, that in some book you'd buy in an airport he would at this very moment reach out and clasp his brother's hand. But Brendan sat still. How could he sit there and nod? *You little fuck, how could you know what it's like?* How could a man who has pushed away every person in his life who ever loved him know anything about losing someone like Rita?

He lifted his coffee cup and studied the small brown moat that had formed in the saucer.

"She had ovarian cancer," he muttered, wanting the words to silence Martin and finding that he regretted the sound of the phrase as it left his mouth. Brutal and dismissive. Maybe it was because a life couldn't be summed up in a rejoinder as easily as a final diagnosis. The words were almost as bad as just HBC, the abbreviation written on a chart when an animal was brought into the clinic off the streets after being struck by a vehicle. Animals snapping at the air, wild with pain and fear and nothing to be done. He felt something like a sob tear off inside him, and tried not to think about the details, how the history of Rita's death could be followed back: One cell with an abnormal program becomes two cells that become the vague abdominal pain that becomes the doctor's visit that becomes the motion required to pick up a ringing telephone, not knowing how it would change everything. *Your wife for you on line two, Dr. Fallon.*

"I didn't know," Martin said, his expression unchanged.

Of course you didn't, he thought as a waitress cleared away the breakfast dishes, Brendan's cup stranded in midair. He studied his brother and wondered how they had gotten to this point. He felt he urgently needed to understand the reason why he was here, with this man, dragging him, following him. Martin, regardless of what he saw, of what he could see, would not take his eyes off him.

"We should get going," Brendan said.

The elevator from the restaurant to the parking garage was silent and swift, a thousand microprocessors striving to eliminate the sensation of g-forces and velocity and terror that should come with any hundred-foot drop down a darkened elevator shaft. Brendan tried to concentrate on the numbered lights flashing as they descended, trying to ignore the sense that Martin was staring at him. Judging him. *You are here because you watch,* he told himself. You are here because you are nothing more than an observer in your life. You watch your wife create a home life for your children that excuses a busy man like you from the day-to-day banalities of their upbringing, unaware that your detachment will mean their absolute indifference to you when she is gone. You watch as your life's work is purchased and dismantled and you are handed a time card and a very large check. The irony, of course, is that all this feels so much like a life being lived, so real that you're completely unaware that you're only watching. At floor twenty-five now, falling at a speed as close to free-fall as you could get without an airplane and a parachute, comfortably nestled in a box that reassures you with the lie that you are not falling, you admit that you still watch, with two cups of coffee in your hands, as your brother staggers off toward a highway—oh, how you had wanted that automatic response to kick in, that protective reflex to be deployed that would leave you winded before you realized you were running. You tell yourself you wanted to be everything that that sprinting man would be—the father who had taken the time to enmesh himself into the messy details of his sons' lives, the brother who forgave, the man who was not so easily and thoroughly embittered that the act of saving his brother was not perfectly instinctual. But you stood there in the parking lot, clutching two cups of take-out coffee. You watch. You watch because you want to see whether Martin is heading for the traffic, whether he is guided by the same dark drive and shares the same impulse that you have never been able to admit in yourself. Brendan looked at Martin, the half-blind architect leaning against a mirrored wall, unaware of their descent, and then turned around to face the opening elevator door.

It began to rain as they pulled into the parking lot of the Château, and in the time it took to park the car, a fierce downpour had begun. Brendan turned off the engine and waited, assuming a squall that began so quickly would blow over in a moment. He stared out the obscured windshield.

Several times that morning, as they'd stood side by side in the bathroom, finishing Martin's shave, Brendan had given his brother the option of staying back at the hotel. If he didn't feel well. If he wasn't up to it. Mom wouldn't know the difference, he said. Each offer was refused. He hadn't known why he'd been so insistent in giving Martin chances to back out, but perhaps he'd sensed something, as Martin slowly became more agitated as they neared their mother's residence. His hands seemed to flutter on his lap, and his eyes, visible now that he had abandoned his sunglasses, seemed intent on focusing on things five or ten feet away, invisible to the rest of the world.

"You okay?"

"Yeah," Martin said unconvincingly.

Brendan pulled opened a couple of heavy institutional doors and entered the reception area. Even with fifteen or so residents waiting to receive visitors, it had an atmosphere that, to Brendan, seemed to be particular to old-age residences: silence and stillness, the laws of thermodynamics muted in accordance with the overall decorating style. Martin, who followed a pace or two behind him, now swiveled his head; his attention seemed to be caught on the large flower arrangement that sat in the middle of the hall.

"Is there some sort of reception desk?"

"We have to sign in"

"You handle it, okay?"

"Uh, sure," Brendan, said. "Are you all right? A nod, as though Martin were trying to swallow a pill without water.

"We're here to see Mrs. Fallon."

"Oh, Mr. Fallon, it's good to see you again. Is your mother expecting you?"

"We called earlier. I'm here with my brother."

"I'll just check the register," the nurse said, and looked over at Martin, whose face twitched into a furtive split-second smile before he ducked behind his brother. Brendan glanced at him over his shoulder, certain that if this had been a bank, the security guards would have unclipped their holsters at this point. But the nurse handled it like a consummate pro, her gaze simply bouncing off Martin and back to him, intuitively understanding Martin was one of those simply fucked-up but essentially harmless types. The brother fresh out of some drug rehab collared into a visit with his mum. A potential disturbance if he were the sole visitor, but accompanied by someone like Brendan, he would be fenced in by familial embarrassment. Split second assessment, years of staffing the reception desk, years of smelling people out from three feet away. Had he still been in business, Brendan would have hired someone like her on the spot. "Here we have it. Oh, she's been a busy lady. You gentleman can wait over there in our solarium. I'll make a call to get her down for you."

"Thank you."

Brendan had been to the Château dozens of times, and while he was for the most part pleased with the home he had secured for his mother, he hadn't yet found a reason to revise his initial dislike of the solarium. The air in the room seemed perpetually damp and several of the panes of glass were obscured by a dun haze of mildew, which, for what he was paying, seemed a little substandard. Still, he reasoned, he couldn't put his mother through the trauma of another move just because of solarium issues. The floor was tiled, not carpeted—an essential part of the setup to encourage the easy movement of wheelchairs—and this detail, along with the fact that the solarium was often deserted, nudged the ambience of the room into the depressing "institutional" category. Perhaps understanding this, the management had tried to remedy the situation by decorating the room with small circular tables and garishly upholstered wing-back chairs straight out of the lobby of a Ramada Inn. It was all well intentioned and utterly confused and he was glad Martin—who had found a chair opposite him and collapsed into it—was in no shape to critique it. He looked around for his mother but saw no one. He smelled Scotchgard and the faint scent of urine and consulted his watch.

Brendan was surprised by their mother's appearance at the entrance to the solarium, sitting in a wheelchair pushed by a nurse's assistant. He looked at his mother in her wheelchair. She wore a white cardigan over her dress, something he could have imagined her wearing at home, which he realized meant a lot to him. After a rapid descent into the incapacities of old age that necessitated selling the house and arranging for her to come here, their mother, it seemed to Brendan, had stopped aging in the last two or three years. Now she sat in the chair with a patrician calm that, Brendan noted, was common among the other residents. He imagined that she could sit this way for hours, then return to her room without a word if she had not been prompted into some form of interaction. There was no pleading when he left, no recriminations that one might expect for not having visited enough. And while it didn't seem entirely like his mother, this equanimity cheered Brendan nonetheless, not just because his mother seemed comfortable but also because it allowed him to think that getting old was not necessarily a harrowing sentence of rattling bed rails and diapers and anguished incoherence, but offered the possibility of a dignified retreat into silence.

The nursing assistant maneuvered the wheelchair into position between the brothers and bent down beside each wheel to engage the hand brakes. She wore a multicolored polyester smock over what appeared to be surgical greens, instantly recognizable to Brendan as the default uniform of the health-care worker. On her left wrist she wore a rubber bracelet, the kind that advertised an adopted cause, usually one's opposition to a specific illness, often cancer. Who *wasn't* against cancer? he thought, already ashamed at his peevishness and wondering what color would signify ovarian. A light blue came to mind, and he didn't know why. The nursing assistant's band was green, and it was only when she finished putting the brakes on the chair and straightened up that he saw the band also had the black triangles and yellow cross that made up the flag of Jamaica.

Brendan stood and went over their mother, bending to give her a quick kiss on the cheek. He looked up at the nursing assistant.

"Thanks," he said to her. "We can take her back."

"I'd like you to stay, Ramona," their mother said, reaching around with her right hand to clasp the younger woman's hand, which lay on her shoulder. Brendan tented his eyebrows and looked at the woman.

"I can stay," Ramona said. "I'll just be over in the corner reading if you need me, Helen."

"Thank you, dear."

"Happy birthday, Mom." Brendan said, and put a bouquet of flowers in her lap.

Brendan motioned for Martin to stand up, but Martin was staring at his mother across the little glass table that separated them. Brendan took a step over to his brother and hooked a middle and index finger under Martin's arm, drawing him to his feet and shepherding him closer. "Mom, I brought someone with me."

"Hi, Mom," Martin said.

"Hello," replied his mother in a tone of polite neutrality, as though greeting an acquaintance in a movie line.

"It's me," Martin said, and moved closer. "It's me, Martin."

"Oh, *Martin.* Do you live here now?"

"In Detroit? No. I'm still in Montreal. But Brendan was coming, so I thought I'd come for once." Martin leaned over to kiss her cheek but instead felt himself pulling away from the distinct ridges of her ear. "I was in an accident."

"Oh, yes. Yes. Are you okay now?" He heard her voice, which sounded raspier and softer than he remembered. The slightest hint of Glasgow still there, at the back of the throat, hanging on. There was nothing to say about her face except that he could not recognize his mother. What have I done for my mother, he asked himself, other than run? He moved closer. He closed his eyes and reached out for her hand.

"Don't cry."

"I'm not crying, Mom. It's just easier with my eyes closed."

"That doesn't sound very promising."

"No, I'm getting better."

"Your brother told me about the trouble you were in."

"I was in the hospital, but I'm out now." He looked around for Brendan and found him standing over them. "But today is about you. Happy birthday". She reached over, the heel of her hand skidding up against his forearm until it found the crook of the elbow. Her thumb and forefinger pinched a small ridge of material.

"Thank you for the flowers. It was so nice to see Sharon again."

"Sharon?" Martin asked.

"She was just here," his mother said, and Brendan nodded.

"Okay," Martin said. "And the girls send their love, too."

"These are nice flowers. Did you get them at Fensters'? Fensters' on Highland always had the best flowers. Orchids, the most delicate things. But orchids have no smell, and *these* smell wonderful." She brought the flowers closer to her and then buried her entire face in the bouquet. It was an indiscriminate and childlike gesture, as though smell were not enough to fully understand *flowers.* She lifted her head, and Brendan could not be sure he didn't see a form of rapture on her face. "Oh, a bouquet from Fensters'. You know I would tease your father that the one disadvantage to always being on holiday during the week of my birthday was that I never got a bouquet from Fensters'."

"I don't think Fensters' is around anymore," Martin said, looking at a shrugging Brendan.

"That's right," their mother replied. "They took that from us."

"I don't understand," Brendan said.

"The blacks. They took everything from us." Brendan cleared his throat and cast a glance at Ramona, who didn't look up from her magazine. "You're father worked so hard, and they burned it down."

Brendan was up now, a hand on both sides of the wheelchair frame, staring down at her. "Mom, come on. We had a good life, Mom. Whatever happened . . ."

"I remember what happened."

"Then you know that Dad rebuilt the business. And it was better than ever."

"They burned us down."

"Lots of black businesses were burned out, too."

"Does that make it better?"

"No."

"Fensters' burned down too. They never reopened."

"Let's talk about something else."

"We should talk about Fensters'," she said, her voice rising in pitch, enough to get Ramona and even the people behind the desk to glance over. "We should talk about Fallon's Electrical."

"Mom, come on."

"Don't 'come on' me. Do you know what it did to your father?" Their mother leaned forward, the flowers almost falling out of her lap. Brendan put out an arm to catch her should she pitch forward. "He was never the same."

"Mom . . ."

"It made him give up on Detroit."

"Mom, we left Highland Park years before the riots."

"We kept the store there."

"But we left. *We* left."

"Would you stop saying that!"

Brendan sat back in the chair and put his hand to his forehead. "I don't know where . . ."

Martin turned to the other two, sensing the novel energy of a family argument without him at the center. He stroked his mother's shoulder.

"Mom, it's okay."

Now their mother fixed on Martin's face. "He's like that. Vietnam." Martin smiled and nodded, understanding.

"Why is it that every problem I have ever had is Vietnam's fault?" Brendan said from his chair.

"Well, something about you changed when you came back."

Brendan was up now, pointing at Martin like a television lawyer, "Something about *him* changed and he never even fucking went."

Their mother grimaced at the language before turning to Martin, "And then there was the marriage. . . ."

"The marriage, the marriage. Okay, I admit it, I made a mistake. But there were some people who got divorced in the seventies who didn't go to Vietnam."

Helen leaned over and whispered to Martin, "I liked your Rita the best." Martin smiled, choosing not to correct her.

"Do you know what happened to me in Vietnam? Do you? I was actually okay. I know that might not fit with what you think must have happened, but there it is. I was happy. I got up in the morning and worked. . . ."

Martin snorted. "*Worked?*"

"I fought; okay, I fought. People shot at me. I shot back. But the people I was with, I would have died for them." He turned to Martin, "I wouldn't expect you to know anything about that."

"Well, if that's all it takes, maybe I'll just napalm another culture to give myself a sense of community." Brendan got up from his chair and walked away. Martin saw Ramona, the nursing assistant, look up again, no doubt familiar with the cadences of little spats and wondering if now was one of those moments to rescue her ward from the loving embrace of family. She paused, watching Martin and his mother. Weighing things, probably.

"Why couldn't your brother be more like you?" His mother said, and Martin looked over his right shoulder for Brendan but found no one. He tried to refocus on his mother. "I knew he'd do something like this," she said, whispering and leaning forward so that their foreheads almost touched.

"Like what? "Martin asked.

"Hurt himself."

Martin held her hand in his. He tried to look into her eyes to see if she knew whom she was talking to. He felt the cuff of her cardigan, the soft wool, which seemed more knowable than the fog of meaning around her.

"Why do you think he'd do that?" Martin asked.

"He could never live down disappointment."

"Who are you talking about, Mom?"

"Your brother."

"Which one of us?"

She paused and shook her hand in front of her face, as though shooing a persistent fly. "Oh, you're the same."

"We're different."

"People imagine they're different. I understand."

"I'm Martin, Mom."

His mother said nothing. The angles of her mouth pulled down and then up, into some sort of expression whose meaning Martin wished he knew, an expression he felt he should know. But, watching her, he realized he didn't know what this expression meant. This small clue to her inside world would disappear and he would forget about it, forget about this moment and his perplexity regarding it. He'd simply never know. Ramona was already at his shoulder, bending over to release the brakes on his mother's chair. She knew.

Chapter 22

"You ready to go?" Martin asked his brother, who rose from the bench he'd been sitting on outside the entrance to the Château. It had taken Martin a good ten minutes to find his way out of the building, and although the pavements were still wet, he'd emerged into a sunny afternoon.

"Yeah," Brendan replied.

"You should go easy on her."

"What?"

"On Mom. She doesn't know what she's saying."

"Look. I just don't like that kind of talk."

"You mean about the riots? *She's demented,* for Christ's sake. She thought Sharon visited her this morning. She doesn't know what she's saying."

"And in front of that assistant—"

"Who, *Ramona*? Ramona didn't give a shit about what Mom said. Ramona understands."

"I don't care what Ramona thinks."

"Then why are you upset? Is it the Vietnam stuff? She doesn't know what she's talking about. She doesn't even know *whom* she's talking to."

"She knows."

She doesn't know, Martin told himself as he heard Brendan's phone begin to ring. His brother answered it with an urgency of someone expecting a call. The deflation in his voice after an expectant "Hello" told Martin it wasn't the person Brendan had hoped for.

Martin walked along ahead, trying to remember the details of Brendan's car, stopping at each car he touched and deciding if this was the one. Nothing was familiar enough to commit to. Only the insides of Brendan's car existed. She had no idea whom she was talking to, Martin repeated as he kept walking. She is demented. She thought Sharon had visited, for Christ's sake. He stopped because his legs suddenly felt weak, a sensation that came upon him so quickly that he thought he would fall, and he held out his right hand to brace himself against the nearest car. From somewhere behind him he heard Brendan's voice, the cadence of a phone call. Speech and silence, a rally with words against some satellite in space. He felt himself breathing hard, his temples damp, and then his heart announced itself with a bailiff-quality knock against his breastbone. His mother knew everything. She knew. Martin stood motionless between cars, lost in what felt like an abyss, and was unable to move. *How could she know*? It didn't matter that she didn't know whom she was talking to; she knew whom she was talking about. Intuition, a mothering instinct, Scot's cynicism—he wanted to curse whatever primeval program it was that survived, thrived even, in his mother's brain when everything else of human value was shutting down. He leaned over the car he had stopped at, trying to catch his breath.

He listened for his brother. Brendan's part of the conversation was reduced to monosyllables—"yes, sure, not really"—something being proposed to him, or a favor being asked. "Sure, don't worry. I know where it is." Something being agreed to. "Bye." He heard the sound of a phone being snapped shut.

"Where's the car?" he asked, fairly certain he couldn't go any farther.

"You're standing next to it," replied Brendan.

The car moved into traffic and accelerated in a way that indicated to Martin that they were on an expressway. He put the visit with his mother out of his mind and turned his head to the window. He wanted to see Detroit again. Darkened towers and empty streets, all of it perfect. A pilgrimage to ground zero, with its cindered shrines and vague memories of what you used to believe in. Of what you were.

He wondered if the Dime Building was still there, or the Ford. He had walked past these buildings countless times as a child, on a sojourn downtown with his hand in his mother's, Brendan on the other side. Both of the buildings—neoclassical monuments to Detroit's might—were Burnham's work, something he'd realized only years after he'd left Detroit and become interested in architecture. And yet he was certain he could remember walking past them and thinking about Burnham. This seemed certain and yet he realized it was impossible.

Maybe the Dime still stood; after all, Detroit had yet to knock down all its old buildings, perhaps pacing itself for the next fifty years of inevitable decline and still seeing some value in the small burst of civic celebrity that accompanied public demolitions. They'd begun tearing things down when he still lived here, and from a distance he'd followed the chain of events associated with every building doomed to destruction: the initial outrage always neatly balanced by the chamber of commerce's call for renewal of the downtown, the injunctions from historical societies, the hearings (accompanied by the ebb and flow of public outrage, the realpolitik of money and influence and exhaustion at the process). Then came the countdown. Once you got to the countdown, the anxiety seemed to ease. And everyone but the most hard-core preservationists would agree that bringing down the buildings—abandoned, given over to vandals and people like Norah's "urban explorers"—felt therapeutic, almost cathartic. People seemed to enjoy watching Detroit die, piece by piece, in clouds of dust after the initial dynamite blast. Micro immolations of a place whose success they'd never really believed, perhaps even begrudged.

He adjusted the car seat, reclining it until it gave that mechanical groan that told him he had reached its limits. He told himself that he'd never wanted to be in a place more than in Detroit at that very minute. Detroit for its lost promise. Detroit for its amnesia. Detroit was his town, hollow-cored and ignored, a simulation site for a neutron bomb. His only regret was never having built something here, something as big and vulgar and Ozymandian as a goddamn consulate. Detroit deserved it as much as he did. He closed his eyes and tried to listen to the engine of the car, but, not being a product of the Motor City, it coursed on in smug and efficient silence. But Detroit was in him now, even without the accompanying machine roar, infusing him with a spirit that no chamber of commerce could understand. He loved Detroit, not just because it gave him his origins but because at certain times in a person's life, a city comes to embody one's mood perfectly. Paris in the springtime, Rio during Carnival, Detroit when your mother's just intimated she always knew you'd try to kill yourself.

The car came to a stop and Brendan turned off the engine. Martin squinted in the midafternoon light, wondering where the reassurances of car-park darkness were.

"Are we at the hotel?"

"No."

"Where are we?"

"The Central Station."

Martin tilted his head and looked at the building. "You know it's closed, right?"

"I know.

"So why are we here?"

"Apparently, we can get in around the back."

Martin laughed. "Around the *back*? It's all back."

"Norah told me. She's here."

"Where?

"Inside. She called me as we were leaving the Château."

"Inside *that*? Oh, this is one of those expedition things. . . ." He felt Brendan nod.

"She said she'd meet us inside."

"What does she want?"

"She just told me where she was."

Martin sat motionless, "You're crazy to go in there. It's abandoned and condemned and it's probably like the Waldorf for crackheads inside."

"I think you should come"

"It's dangerous. You don't . . ."

"Your daughter's inside. Are you coming?"

"You'd go in there?"

"I want to go in, yeah."

"Why?"

"I want to see the inside of that building. I'd like to see Norah again. You should go in."

"I can't."

"Tell yourself that it's just a fascinating building, a historic building, that's all."

"No, you don't understand."

"I understand." Martin heard the sound of the car door

opening. "I understand perfectly. I don't think you understand; your children will walk away from you."

"What has that got to do with anything?"

"That's what this is about."

"Why do you say that?"

"Because that's what everything is about. They will walk away from you."

"That's their choice."

"Stop making their choice so easy."

"I think you're projecting." The car door closed in response. Martin struggled to undo the seat belt before pushing the door open. "You know this car is going to get stolen if you leave it here; you know that, right?" He scanned the area that Brendan seemed to have walked into—scrub overgrowth and a crumbling curbside—but could not locate him.

"I don't care," said Brendan, from what sounded like twenty feet away. Martin turned to face the sound and found him.

Martin slammed the door closed. "I'm not going to wait here for the carjacking, okay?"

"I didn't ask you to wait. I asked you to come with me."

"This is nuts."

"I don't care about the car."

"But we'll have to walk home." Martin stepped over something the size of a cinder block or a small carcass. "This is serious. The car will be gone."

"Then we'll walk, okay? Come on, we're late," Brendan said, and stopped walking, waiting as Martin caught up to him.

"You can't be late for a building like this—"

"Do you remember being in it?"

"Not much. I remember the waiting room. Lots of light, big space."

"She said at the southeast corner there would be an opening in the fence."

"Just keep an eye out for cops. I don't want to get arrested," Martin said as he stumbled on the uneven terrain. He kept his hands stretched out on either side to help him balance. Brendan stopped suddenly, and Martin, walking behind and paying attention to the ground under him, ran into his back.

"This is it," Brendan said, and Martin heard the wheeze of chain link being tugged repeatedly. "Step through."

Martin complied and stepped into the yard, and that was when he caught sight of the structure. Invisible a moment before, it was now mountainous before him. For a second he thought he could discern the Beaux-Arts details, the facade that had long ago begun to fissure and crack and whose features were now in open revolt. But this was a flash of recognition, and as he stared at the building, he was surprised to see how amorphous it became, as though the details seen a moment before were nothing more than a memory, and that the memory was more real than the building he was looking at.

"I remember it now," he said to his brother.

They walked around the perimeter of the lot, along the inside of the fence, until Brendan noticed movement close to a corner of the building. He saw a hand raised in the air, motioning him closer.

"Are you Brendan?" a tiny woman said as she waved him over. Even as they approached, she continued to scan the area around her. "Come on," she said." There are CP police everywhere." She spoke with an accent that Brendan thought sounded Eastern European and that made talk of rushed entry and police evasion—whoever the "CP police" were—sound all the more convincing. They squeezed through an opening in a door that looked like an ax had created it and then stepped into darkness so deep, it made Brendan reconsider the wisdom of coming to a place like this. She snapped on a flashlight and they followed the bouncing circle of light, ducking under spiderwebs toward other doorways, registering glimpses of ruin and deep silence around them, reminding Brendan of undersea camera footage from the *Titanic.*

The tiny woman, whose arms were comprised of small ropes of muscle, marched ahead of him through the darkness and they arrived at a larger and better-lit antechamber, where Norah stood, shouldering her camera. Her attention was directed to filming two other people who were adjusting what looked to Brendan like climbing equipment gathered at their feet, coiled nylon rope and metal loops and clamps. Brendan approached, with Martin behind him; the climbers looked up, but Norah was still too concentrated on filming to notice. When Brendan put his hand on her shoulder, she jumped.

"I thought you were the police," she said, hugging her uncle. Martin stood in new shadows cast by Norah's light, watching the two embrace.

"I brought Martin," Brendan said. Norah turned to face him.

"Didn't think you'd come."

"I wanted to see this," Martin said. "I wanted to see what you do."

Norah introduced the two of them to the people in climbing gear. The young woman with the build of a gymnast was introduced as Luisa, and as she shook Brendan's hand, he could imagine her scaling the wall without aid. Next came her bearded friend Carl, who looked like he needed the rope. Another hand jutted out at Brendan, ready to be shaken.

"This is Stefan," Norah said, and Brendan's hand was locked in a chalky grip he immediately recognized had potential crushing force. This was defused, partially, by Stefan's smile. Martin came next, quietly nodding a hello to the group.

"Are you feeling better?" Luisa asked Martin, putting a hand on his shoulder. Martin stepped back from the question and the gesture, and simply replied "No."

Sensing the awkwardness, Norah turned to Brendan and asked, "Was Grandma wearing the sweater I brought her?"

"It was you," Martin murmured as Brendan described her resplendent in her cardigan.

"Who wears a sweater in July?" asked Carl.

The sense of light and air and sound. Sensations that were the substance or precursor to a memory of space. All registered in some type of memory that must not have adhered to the rules that govern other memories, as these were memories that denied immediate recollection but were instead incidentally evoked in that same way that a sense of the Michigan Central Station became apparent at that moment for Martin. He wondered how much of what he was feeling was due to this place and how much was borrowed from impressions of Union Station in Toronto and Grand Central, surrogate details stripped away and reconstructed, called into service for the human tendency to span the gaps of what was missing. Model making. An architecture inside his head. Martin's gaze drifted to the ceiling and then climbed down along the brickwork until it rested on the group of people in front of him.

"What are you doing here?" he asked.

"We were looking to get up on the roof," Stefan replied, "just above the waiting area." He pointed to a breach where the wall and ceiling would have met. The plaster had fallen away, along with the bricks underneath, and a small rhombus of sky was visible between the beams of supporting metalwork.

"You're okay to climb it?" Luisa asked, examining the wall as though she were plotting her footholds. She frowned.

"It's doable, very doable," said Stefan.

Brendan asked, "What if the police come when you're in midair?"

"Then they get their ropes and come up and get me," Stefan said, and smiled in a way that told Brendan he'd made this kind of calculation before.

The main waiting room was an enormous space, and it seemed larger to Brendan for the wreckage it contained. Garbage lay clustered in mysterious rows that ran the length of the hall. Graffiti scrawls and what appeared to be halfhearted attempts at arson marked the walls. A pigeon flew in a tight circular pattern in the vaulted space above them. Doors had been smashed or lifted out of their hinges, radiator covers had been removed, and moldings had been hacked away, all examples to Brendan of vandal erosion, the minimalism that anarchy demanded.

He could remember standing with his parents in the tumult of a crowd, amid the sound of footsteps echoing in the plaza. He recalled sunlight passing into the building. The hall was a testament to debauched beauty, and Brendan could not decide if the knowledge of what it had once been made him feel better or worse.

Luisa backed away and looked at the wall again. She shook her head. "I'm going to try to find my way up a back stairwell. Any takers?"

"I'll go with you," said Brendan.

He followed Luisa out of the waiting room and back into the darkness of a warren of rooms that he worried might offer no way out. But Luisa negotiated her way through the clutter and darkness with an ease that relieved his anxiety.

"Have you been here before?"

"A few times," she replied without looking back. She pushed open a door, revealing a stairwell. She turned and looked at him with a smile that would be described as impish, even in Prague or Sofia.

"Is this your hobby?"

She shook her head. "I was an architect," she said. "Before. And I want to see these buildings before they're gone. But it's good to hang out with people like these; they help you get into a lot of places you wouldn't otherwise go."

The stairwell reeked, its walls coated with thick layers of carbonized grime. He was worried that they would stumble upon a body. Luisa was undaunted and climbed, two steps at a time. By the end of the second flight, he was beginning to feel a little winded and needed to stop, choosing to rest with his hand on the stanchion, trying to affect a look of wariness at continuing, should she turn around and see him not climbing. He watched her, and for a moment he thought that she reminded him of Rita. Her hair was similarly short and she did have a certain energy to her step that was familiar. But as he studied her continuing up the stairs, he began to enumerate the ways in which she did not look like Rita. It struck him as an odd ritual need, this declaration and its immediate rebuttal, the reassurances of loneliness.

"You should have told him you were an architect."

"You think so?" she replied, herself a touch breathless now. They had come to the end of the stairwell, and she reared and drew back her foot.

"Maybe not," Brendan said as she kicked open the door to daylight. They stepped out of the stairwell and onto the roof. He stayed close to the stairwell doorway while Luisa began to explore the rooftop on her own, stepping gingerly and stopping just short of a hole that he expected led down to the waiting room. He watched as she surveyed the rooftop, taking out a camera and snapping a few pictures of the gaping hole she stood next to. She looked up, saw him watching her, and seemed embarrassed.

"It is a very big hole, worthy of several pictures," she explained.

He'd expected the sight of Detroit from this height to disappoint him, to be as foul and ugly as anything from street level. But as he stepped farther out onto the rooftop, he felt nothing of what he'd expected. He looked at Detroit for the first time in years without needing to have an emotion. He felt free of the bonds of nostalgia and despair. He held his right hand up to shield his eyes from the sunshine. In this light, it looked quite beautiful.

Brendan and Luisa disappeared just as Stefan began to climb what remained of a pillar in the corner of the waiting room. Martin could not imagine anyone being able to scale such a surface, but Stefan advanced upward, buglike and methodical, with Norah filming his every move. Martin moved up until he was beside his daughter, whose attention was still focused on the young man inching up the wall. He wanted to say something to her, not particularly to apologize or explain himself as much as be near her and have a moment where talk and apologies could occur. They could talk. They could understand each other. He heard a sound like the clearing of her throat and he turned to it, but she was rapt, neck extended and her gaze directed upward. He wanted to reach out and touch her but did not. He wished that she would turn around, that she would put the camera down. They could talk, he thought, without any of the intrusions that always seemed to come between them. He would apologize then. But she was facing in the other direction, and already farther away from him. It made him want to leave.

Above them, Stefan continued to advance, and it wasn't long before he had disappeared altogether. A short silence was broken by the *thwack* of a rope dropping to the ground from above.

Carl, whom Martin had forgotten about, called out from the darkness, "Would you like to see it up close?"

"Me? I can't climb up there."

"We can hoist you up. We have a harness."

"I don't think that's a good idea," Norah said.

"No, I want to," Martin replied, and despite Norah's protests, he stepped into the harness, which cinched around his waste and between his legs. After a briefing from Carl, Martin readied himself.

The pull of the ropes brought back memories of the Dunes, the poolside physio, and Hoyer lifts and the sense of his body as weight that needed constant lifting. Stefan shouted down instructions, telling him to try to maintain his balance with his feet facing the wall as he was being pulled up, but he began to spin slowly, and as his weight made him swing back and forth, he ended up brushing up against the wall with his side and then his back.

"Steady yourself," Stefan called out from above.

Martin uttered a silent *Yes* to himself and raised his right arm to brace against the next impact.

He saw the physical evidence of decay, the plaster rotted and gone and the herringbone arrangement of the underlying brickwork. Architecture is a sustained argument with gravity, and gravity will always win. He held out his hand and touched the brick, which was cold with moisture. He looked down and estimated he was a good twenty feet in the air, spinning away from the wall, the volume of the room enlarging below him. He remembered how vast and beautiful a space it had been. Now he was faced with the wall again, a little wrecking ball of a man swinging toward a particularly fragile-looking section of it. A grunt as he made impact.

"Are you okay?" asked Stefan.

"I'm fine."

In the air, rising with every tug of the rope below him, he began to think of Melnikov's house, the space in the main rooms, the salon and the study, and how he had come to meet the great architect and found a little man who had been hiding there for forty years. He remembered leaving the house with that vague sense that a twenty-two year-old has of being let down for reasons he can't quite yet understand. It takes a life to understand that what he felt was not merely disappointment but also a nascent despair, the desire to cry for the knowledge that what he'd thought was integrity was nothing more than being permitted to build one's own cage, one's own crypt, and be oblivious to the fact that you had done so. *You are a fool,* he thought, remembering Melnikov and finishing the tea that Anna had brewed and wanting to run from the place. He reached out again to touch the frayed plaster, but he misjudged the distance and tipped in the direction of the wall. He heard a gasp below that he thought sounded like Norah, but then he righted himself and felt another pull as he was drawn closer to the ceiling. *You are a fool.* When he had returned to Montreal after the visit to Moscow and described his experiences to Sharon, he did not mention the visit, and when she asked, he denied that it had ever occurred. Denied he had ever met Melnikov. Some bureaucrat had interfered, he had told her, because this could have been true, because this preserved some meaning that he had carried forward and come to believe as the truth. Lanctot had never written about the visit, nor had they discussed it—whether that was due to disappointment on Lanctot's part or merely pure bafflement was never clear. Melnikov cowering in his palace had been their secret to share and they hadn't broken confidence.

He was floating now. From this height and angle, he would have thought that he'd have a unique view of the waiting room, but the space would not come to him and he assumed it must be the darkness or dust or just his fatigue. With his right hand, he reached out, this time past the limits of vision, into the darkness to the left of him, digging through the shadows until he felt the sudden rebuke of pain as his fingers jammed against the masonry wall. He twisted away and wanted to be let down, but he was being hoisted farther up into the vault of the waiting room, into the darkness that now seemed so obvious and deep and irrevocable.

The palm of his right hand skidded along the waiting room wall as he tried to balance himself in midair. The pain from contact with the wall made Martin remember opening that desk drawer and finding what he'd written about Melnikov. Not an article or even a valedictory, but a suicide note. He remembered reading the last page and then staring at the model that sat on the desk, and almost before he was able to register his action, his right fist had caved in the ceiling of the Melnikov pavilion. He sat before it, his wrist protruding from of the model like the tail of some decimating comet. After the initial blow, it was a matter of seconds before the rest was splinters and pieces. At the time, it struck Martin as odd that something he believed he treasured could in an instant be erased without a sense of loss or regret. *I created this. I can destroy this.*

Martin had been pulled up to where Stefan waited at the breach of the ceiling. An extended arm swung toward him, which Martin found and grabbed onto, and in one movement he was pulled to the outside, squinting in the daylight, kneeling on the roof above the waiting room. Martin, trailing the climbing ropes from the harness he wore, struggled to his feet and tried to orient himself on the plateau of the roof. This part of the station was only three or four stories high, but a person could still see the towers of the city from here. Chain link and the scrubland green of Roosevelt Park lay below him. He tried to look at the city, remembering that the city should have been *here,* clustering around the station, bustling, but instead of sprawling toward Corktown, the city had expanded toward the northeast and the station was effectively abandoned long before the last train left. He put his hands in front of his face and then looked out to the city. He could see now; he saw everything, including a sector of sky darkened by what he now knew was his blindness, the sun in eclipse, the city in darkness.

"This place is hard to get to," he heard Stefan say, and tried to find the younger man but could not. Martin turned and moved toward the point where Roosevelt Park emerged in his vision, kept from him by a threshold that he recognized was the building's edge. Behind him, eighteen floors of what had once been someone's beautiful intention continued to rot in the summer sunshine, and he did not feel this was a shame or an unfair judgment or anything other than a place that people chose not to return to. This was what things came to. He looked at the tower and he was aware that the left side of it was freshly gone, already demolished for him. He turned back to the edge and wondered if this was despair, just that understanding of emptiness, the kind of silence one experiences inside a car on the side of the highway on winter nights.

He swam in the late-afternoon heat and Melnikov stepped out of this curtained darkness as though this rooftop were his studio and he had plans he intended to share. But the old man offered nothing more, no warning about what is to come. No words of wisdom about the choices to be made, about what must be left behind.

"You are useless," Martin muttered.

And with this, Melnikov was gone, leaving Martin staggering through empty space. And it was only with the specter of the architect gone that Martin realized that he had been wrong about his subject and himself; where he himself had faltered, Melnikov had only ever prevailed: built according to his ideals, survived the ruinous envy of his colleagues, outlasted an epic foe. He had refused to leave and accepted his fate with an equanimity that, as a young man, Martin Fallon had mistaken for servility and, as an older man, he'd mistaken for despair. He remembered tea in the salon that day in Moscow, the condescension he'd felt for a man who had remained faithful to every meaningful impulse.

"Useless, useless," he said again. Stefan turned around at the sound.

It was weakness that brought him to the line that separated the building from the greenery of the park below, a form of weakness that bent his knees and pulled him to the edge, another failure of the argument against gravity that sent him tipping. Beyond the edge of the building he could see more clearly what remained of Roosevelt Park's green expanse, his world divided into night and day. Standing there, forty feet below, was his daughter—a glimpse only, a flashbulb image that echoed amid the darkness—staring up at him with nothing less than horror, and he wanted to step back, because nothing meant more to him than undoing this. But he could not. Gravity cannot be deceived. Gravity wins, regardless of the onlookers' horror. He saw his daughter's face again but could not tell if it will be the remembered face of her as a child or that last look of horror that will haunt him. Norah. His arms extended and the wind was kicked from his lungs and Norah was gone again. And now he was as good as blind, the world turned liquid and streaming by, and he wanted to say he understood, but no words arrived, nothing except a force doubling him over and driving him back up to the ledge and hands like the beaks of birds fighting for a grip of his shirt and the pain of a harness cutting at his hips. Finally, when everything became still, there was the almost unbearable brightness of the midday sun and familiar shadows that moved among the rays of sunlight and the terrible pain of that next, first full breath.

Acknowledgments

Several books were particularly important to me in the process of writing this book: *The Needs of Strangers* by Michael Ignatieff (Picador 2001); *Melnikov: Solo Architect in Mass Society* by S. Frederick Starr (Princeton University Press, 1981); *Konstantin S Meln'nikov and the Construction of Moscow,* Mario Fosso and Maurizio Meriggi (Skira, 2000); *Body and Building Essays on the Changing Relation of Body and Architecture,* Editors George Dodds and Robert Tavernor, (MIT Press 2002); *Questions of Perception-Phenomenology of Architecture,* Steven Holl, Juhani Pallasmaa and Alberto Pérez-Gómez. (William Stout Publishers, 2006)

Thank you to the Canadian Centre for Architecture for granting me access to archival material related to Konstantin Melnikov, specifically Richard Pare's photographs of Melnikov House.

Thanks to my agent, Denise Bukowski, for advice and forward motion. I was fortunate to find an editor like Erika Goldman at Bellevue Literary Press who shared a vision for the book—my thanks to her and everyone at BLP.

Most of all, thank you to Florence, Niall, Julia, and Tom for your love and support.

Bellevue Literary Press is devoted to publishing literary fiction and nonfiction at the intersection of the arts and sciences because we believe that science and the humanities are natural companions for understanding the human experience. With each book we publish, our goal is to foster a rich, interdisciplinary dialogue that will forge new tools for thinking and engaging with the world.

To support our press and its mission, and for our full catalogue of published titles, please visit us at blpress.org.

Bellevue Literary Press
New York